Drewry cannot live with her deception any longer.

Chase took her in his arms and held her tight. "I'm sorry, Drewry," he breathed. "So sorry to have shouted at you that way."

Drewry returned his hug. "It's all right, Chase," she said, comforting him as she would have one of the children. "It'll be all right. You'll see. . ."

She felt, rather than heard, his heaving sigh. "I'm so grateful for you, Drewry. No matter how badly I've behaved or how cruelly I've spoken to you, you've been a . . .loyal friend."

He pushed back the hood of her raincoat, then gently cupped her face in his hands. "I'm a very fortunate man to have a friend to share all my troubles with—without fear of judgment or scorn."

Then, softly, so softly that she scarcely felt the pressure of his lips, Chase dropped a kiss on her forehead. "Yes, I'm a lucky man . . . and that's the truth."

Truth. . . . truth . . . truth. The word echoed in her head, spinning and tumbling and leaving her stunned and breathless. This was the moment she had been dreading, the inevitable moment. It was time to tell Chase the truth.

CARA MCCORMACK's writing career spans nearly two decades. Her byline has appeared thousands of times in national and local magazines and newspapers. She teaches writing at her local community college, and speaks frequently on writing-related topics for government, education, and private agencies. The author of dozens of novels, Cara lives in Maryland with her husband and children.

Drewry's Bluff

Cara McCormack

The Road to Truth

Heartsong Presents

DEDICATION

To my husband, for his support and encouragement,
To my children, for their cooperation
and understanding,
To my Lord and Savior, who called me to write.

A note from the Author:
I love to hear from my readers! You may write to me at
the following address: **Cara McCormack**
Author Relations
P.O. Box 719
Uhrichsville, OH 44683

ISBN 1-55748-772-3

DREWRY'S BLUFF

Cover illustration by Kathy Arbuckle.

PRINTED IN THE U.S.A.

prologue

Baltimore
Autumn, 1844

Little Drewry Sheffield had missed her mama and papa nearly every minute of every day since they'd died, months earlier. A snake had frightened the roan mares that pulled her father's grand carriage, overturning it and pinning her parents beneath its big, iron-rimmed wheels.

She wished they were here with her now, to explain why she had to sit in this huge room, filled with black-suited, stern-looking men. She hugged her rag doll tightly and met her uncle's clear blue gaze.

"Come sit here on my lap, my precious Drew-girl," James said, smiling gently as he patted his thigh. "You look like a scared rabbit, and there's absolutely no reason for you to be afraid."

Drewry snuggled against his big, broad chest. The steady *thump, thump, thump* of his heart comforted her. "Uncle James," she whispered, "why are we here in this big, dark room? And when can we go home?"

He'd be honest with her; he always had been. She remembered the morning of her fifth birthday, when Muffin disappeared. Everyone at Plumtree Orchards had told her, in sweet sing-songy voices, that her pup had run off to live a happier life in puppy heaven.

But James, seventeen at the time, had waited until the sun was high in the sky, then he'd taken her hand and led her along the banks of the Gunpowder River. There, on a ridge overlooking the valley, he had told her point-blank that her dog had died of distemper. "You're not a baby anymore," he'd said. "You deserve to know the truth."

She'd never forgotten that. Many times since then, she had returned to the place Uncle James had dubbed "Drewry's Bluff," since it was there that he hadn't bluffed her about the truth. She wished she could go there now.

"What's going on?" she asked again. "Why do they all look so *angry?*"

"Hush," he soothed softly, patting her slender back. "See there? Mr. Taylor is about to call this meeting to order, at long last."

Dubiously, Drewry eyed Mr. Taylor, a man she'd known her whole life. He and his family had taken dozens of Sunday dinners at the massive mahogany table in the elegant Sheffield dining room. Usually, he had a friendly grin and a mischievous wink for her. But not today. On this bleak, rainy morning, his long, narrow face seemed paler than usual, and the dark, bushy brows above his blue eyes were drawn together in a frown. Drewry couldn't decide if he were angry or sad, and couldn't decide why he'd be either . . .

In fact, every man in the room wore an expression similar to Mr. Taylor's, Drewry noted. Sweet old Mr. Bartell, who sneaked her a chip of rock candy each time she stood with her mother at the counter of his general store, wouldn't meet Drewry's eyes. And Pastor Carter, whose friendly smile never failed to produce one of her own, wasn't smiling now. Why, even Mr. Mossman, who always had a red lollipop waiting for her when she went with her father to the bank, was scowling. She felt small and helpless . . . and very frightened.

Drewry hugged her doll tighter still and squeezed her eyes shut tight. *Sweet Jesus*, she prayed silently, fervently, *please get me out of this scary place!* She held her breath and waited for the magic of God's awesome power to transport her to the cozy comfort of her room. But she wasn't really surprised, when she opened her eyes, to find herself still in the dim, stuffy office . . .

Her mama had told her time and again that if she was very, very good and prayed very, very hard, the Lord would fill each and every one of her needs. Well, she'd been as good as she knew how to be. And she'd prayed, harder than she'd ever prayed in her whole life. Yet God hadn't brought her mama and papa back. Drewry believed His refusal meant she wasn't good enough, hadn't prayed hard enough, to be worthy of His answer.

Joshua Taylor cleared his throat. "I think it's time we get on with the reading of the Last Will and Testament . . ."

The men sat straighter in the red velvet wing chairs that surrounded the lawyer's large oak desk. A rustle of paper whispered through the otherwise silent room as he slid a one-page letter from a white envelope. Drewry knew who'd written it, for she recognized the dark scrawl of her father's powerful hand.

"'To whom it may concern,'" the lawyer began reading. "'In the event of the simultaneous deaths of George Ethan Sheffield and Margaret Mary Sheffield, we, being of sound minds and bodies, do hereby instruct Joshua Taylor, trusted friend and attorney, to dispose of our worldly possessions as follows . . .'"

Taylor stopped, cleared his throat, glanced once around the room. His gaze lingered for a moment on the wide, long-lashed eyes of the child who shuddered involuntarily when he continued reading. "'It is our wish that James Johnson Sheffield shall be executor of our estate and guardian of our only child, Drewry Margaret. All assets and monies now held by First Freetown Bank and Trust shall be made available to him as he deems fit and proper to ensure the financial success of Plumtree Orchard Plantation and all other Sheffield holdings listed herewith, in order that our daughter shall be guaranteed a secure future . . .'"

Mr. Mossman inhaled sharply, and Drewry's gaze lighted on him. Why did he seem so upset? Why did he look so very angry? "What does it all mean, Uncle James?" she whispered, leaning still closer against his broad chest.

"Shhh, Drew-girl," James cautioned. "I'll explain on the way home."

With the unabashed scrutiny of youth, Drewry studied her only relative's handsome face and lively blue eyes. The honesty and affection she saw there eased her mind. Yes, she'd be quiet, because Uncle James had asked her to. She'd do anything, *anything* for Uncle James.

He'd always been her favorite grown-up. He seemed to understand better than other adults the fears and yearnings of a child's heart. Perhaps it was because he'd been born a full ten years after her father and, being the "baby" of the family, had been protected from life's burdens and responsibilities—first by his parents, then by his big brother George. Perhaps it was because he'd only recently turned eighteen himself that he lived life like a carefree boy. Whatever the reason, Drewry sensed she could trust her uncle. So, yes, she'd save her questions for the hour-long ride home.

The men who had gathered to witness the reading of her parents' will moved to a spot near the window. "What was George thinking, leaving his estate in the hands of a ne'er-do-well like James?"

"Now, now," soothed Pastor Carter, "James means well. He's . . . well, he's a happy-go-lucky sort, is all. Besides," he added, "I don't imagine George really believed James would be taking on such a responsibility so soon."

"You've got that right," the lawyer agreed. "Why, George and Margaret were barely thirty when that carriage overturned." Joshua Taylor shook his head. "Surely they expected to live to a ripe old age . . . James, too."

Amos Mossman snorted. "He's a hail-fellow-well-met, that's

what James is. Why, the boy will likely squander George's entire fortune within a year." He pointed a bony finger at the group. "You mark my words!"

His eyes widened with surprise when he glanced around the room and caught Drewry looking at him. "Goodness!" he whispered hoarsely. "The child's heard every word we've said."

Mossman stepped away from the group and went to Drewry. Crouching, he put his hands on her narrow shoulders. "Drewry, my dear," he said, "everything is going to be all right. You'll see." He gave her shoulders a little squeeze. "But if you ever have a problem . . . of any kind . . . come tell me about it, and I promise I'll help in any way I can."

Drewry nodded, but she didn't understand his concern—what "problem" he was talking about, or what "help" he could possibly be, since her Uncle James had promised to take care of her, always . . .

Mossman rejoined his cohorts, still huddled near the window. They were her parents' friends. She'd known them all her life. So Drewry smiled politely, though their whispers and head-shaking sent shivers up her spine.

She searched for her Uncle James, and found him in the outer office, laughing and chatting with Mr. Taylor's pretty young secretary. He sent a merry wink Drewry's way when he spotted her, and immediately, a sense of relief flooded over her.

God couldn't love her, of that Drewry was sure. He'd proven that when He didn't bring her mama and papa back. She must be a very bad girl indeed if even Sweet Jesus, who loved *all* the little children, didn't love her enough to answer such an important prayer. Still, she pondered, she couldn't be all *that* bad . . .

Not if someone as wonderful as her Uncle James loved her.

one

Freetown, Maryland
October, 1868

"Don't you dare contradict me, you ungrateful hussy!" James Sheffield snarled as he raised his hand.

Drewry shrank back from the tall, black-bearded man who reeked of whiskey and cigars. "Uncle James, I can't . . . You can't . . ."

"I can and you will!" He let his arm drop heavily when Drewry sprang back out of his reach.

Accustomed to her uncle's drinking bouts, Drewry knew that his intoxicated state would prevent him from pursuing her. This time, however, like a trapped bird, she huddled against the massive walnut sideboard, her blue calico dress and layers of white petticoats billowing about her slender body like a cloud.

"After all I've done for you!" he roared, his words slurring. "Now, don't you go hidin' on me, girl. I need you to save the estate."

"Uncle, I'm grateful to you for raising me, but I will not marry Porter Hopkins," she said, putting as much determination into her words as she could muster. Her body stiffened. "Not even to save Plumtree Orchards."

"He won you as his bride, fair and square."

Drewry gasped and felt the bile rise in her throat. "You mean you . . . gambled me away at a poker game, like a cow or a donkey?"

"You got that right."

He lurched toward her again. For the first time in her life, Drewry was truly afraid of her uncle. Seeing an opportunity to escape, she sprang from behind the sideboard, grabbing a heavy, silver soup ladle as she went. She ducked his blow as she dashed past the walnut table and hid behind the open door leading to the butler's pantry.

"Don't come any closer! I'm warning you!" she cried, brandishing the soup ladle like a weapon.

"Sweetheart, surely you don't want your daddy's fruit plantation to go to Hopkins and his good-for-nothin' relatives," Sheffield wheedled, his voice suddenly as soft as melted wax. "Once you're legally Mrs. Porter Hopkins, that ol' coot 'll give me back the deed . . ."

"Stay away!"

Drewry knew her uncle's drunken tricks. If he couldn't get his way through anger, he sweet-talked. Usually she humored him, listening to his wild ramblings about the War until Old Jeb took him off to bed. Tonight, she was having none of it.

"He's coming to get you at noon. I'm tellin' you, girl, be ready—if you know what's good for you."

Suddenly, the red, puffy face of Porter Hopkins flashed before Drewry's eyes. Why, the man practically lived in the saloon! Even the thought of the lout sickened her. She recalled the tobacco juice stains in his mottled beard and his foul, disgraceful language. She shuddered. Marry one of the Freetown's low-life gamblers? Never!

"I *won't* marry him. You can't make me. I'm over twenty-one."

"We'll just see about that."

James snatched the key to the dining room door sitting atop the lace doily on the sideboard. In a heartbeat, before Drewry could jump from her hiding place on the other side of the long, narrow room, he stepped outside the heavy door, pulled it shut behind him, and locked it.

As the iron key creaked in the lock, Drewry imagined the sound of a Yankee jailor locking up a Confederate in his cell.

She ran and pounded on the door.

"Uncle, for mercy's sake," she wailed, genuinely frightened now, "don't make me marry a man I don't love!"

"Oh, hush your weeping, girl. You don't have a beau anyway. Who'd want an old maid like you? You're twenty-four, for cryin' out loud. Just thank God someone will take you. Your daddy would have wanted you to marry."

With her palms outstretched, Drewry slid down the door and crumpled into a heap on the pine wood floor. She crouched there, sobbing into her soft cotton skirts. She shivered as she heard her uncle's cane tapping unevenly down the hallway, heading toward the library . . . and his seemingly never-ending whiskey supply. The eerie *tap, tap, tapping* echoed in the high stairwell as he limped away.

In all her years, Drewry had never felt such deep and utter abandonment. Its icy fingers tightened around her stomach. Her horror at Uncle James's cruelty turned into despair. A raw grief overwhelmed her. He was right. She was an old maid. No one wanted her . . .

೩

Drewry checked the brass timepiece perched on the mantel of the white marble fireplace. Two hours past midnight. How long had she lain there, weeping, before falling into exhausted slumber? she wondered, scrambling to her feet. It wouldn't do any good to pray. She knew that by now. No, she'd wasted enough time, precious time, and now she'd have to work quickly if she were to escape marriage to Porter Hopkins.

She eased the window open. The beveled glass panes distorted the bright light of the moon that burnished the dark apple and pear trees. She lifted her hands to either side of her mouth and drew a deep breath. Moments later an owl's cry keened over the dusty yard and filtered back to the servants' quarters, near the barn. Three times she mimicked the owl's cry—the code she and Old Jeb had been using for years whenever she needed his help with her uncle.

And she had needed the faithful servant's help more times than she cared to remember.

Lieutenant Colonel James Sheffield hadn't been the same since he returned from the Civil War. The loving uncle who had reared Drewry since her parents' death had, for all intents and purposes, perished alongside his men on the battlefield at Gettysburg.

Oh, his *body* hadn't died. Instead, it appeared that he had lost his *soul,* she thought bitterly. He still blamed himself for bad decisions that led to the bloody slaughter of so many Confederates under his command. He'd come home a haunted man—his hair gone gray, his left foot half shot away, his face scarred, and nearly blind in one eye.

He often woke, screaming in the night. Unable to live with himself, he sought solace in the golden elixir of a whiskey bottle, trying to hold at bay all the demons that tortured him.

Drewry knew that her uncle had gambled away much of her inheritance at The Silver Dollar Saloon, playing poker with Porter Hopkins and other lay-abouts who were too busy gambling and drinking to tend their crops. Two years before, her old friend, banker Amos Mossman, had told her there was too little money left, and warned her to hide a goodly sum of cash among her personal belongings. Thankfully, she'd followed his advice!

A gentle rapping on the window startled her from her reverie. Peering outside, she saw the familiar form of Old Jeb— trusted friend, farmhand, and former slave.

"Jeb! I'm locked in! He's forcing me to marry Porter Hopkins in the morning!"

"Don't you worry none, Miss Drew," he whispered. "I'll scout out the house and see what Mr. James be up to."

Minutes later, Drewry heard Jeb turn the key in the dining room door. With a great sob, she flung herself against his tall, wiry frame.

"There, there," Jeb crooned as he patted her awkwardly, respectfully distancing himself from her petite figue. "The Good Lord ain't gonna 'bandon you in your hour of need. Mr. James be passed out on the liberry couch."

Drewry pulled away and wiped her tears with the back of her hand. "Will you drive me to the train station, Jeb?"

"'Course I will, Miss Drew. He ain't no match for you, the likes of Porter Hopkins. He be one mean man. He go to church on Sunday, go whoopin' it up with his drinkin' buddies on Monday."

Drewry touched the old man's shoulder. Even through his thick cotton shirt she could feel the scars left by the lashes of many whips. "Thank you, dear friend," she whispered, then gave a shudder of revulsion. "I certainly don't want to be a slave of that ol' coot."

"No, ma'am. Ain't right for no one to be owned by another. We is all chil'ren of God. Now you go on upstairs an' pack yo' bags whilst I get the carriage ready."

Drewry threw Jeb a small, sad smile as she slipped out of the dining room. She tiptoed down the hallway, past the library, and up the wide staircase, hardly daring to breathe until she reached her bedroom.

There, she dragged her tapestry valise from under the bed and hefted it onto her feather-stuffed comforter. Biting back tears, she threw open the doors of the chiffonier and rooted through her dresses. Velvet, silk, taffeta, brocade—all beautiful gowns, expensive gowns. But she'd have to leave most of them behind.

Quickly, she slipped into a green and gold tartan, a good traveling outfit. She wanted to travel far, far away. Far from the fleshy, sweaty hands of Porter Hopkins and the terrors of her uncle's post-War madness. She stuffed as many dresses, skirts, and shirtwaists into the valise as would fit.

Next she opened her rosewood jewelry box and picked out the pieces of the jewelry she'd inherited from her mother. The ivory cameo had come over from England with the family. The ruby necklace and earbobs had been her father's wedding gift to her mother. Fighting back another flood of tears, she slipped on the jewelry. She didn't want to take any chances on thieves rifling though her valise in the train's baggage car.

Jeb suddenly appeared in her doorway, quiet as a ghost. "You ready, Miss Drew?" he whispered.

Almost as an afterthought, she crammed a pair of slippers, an extra pair of button-up boots, and a two-hooped petticoat into the valise. Slamming it, she fastened the lock.

Jeb hoisted it off the bed. "We'll leave from the gateway so's Mr. James don't hear us . . . though he be dead to the world, far as I can tell."

As Jeb tiptoed down the servants' staircase, Drewry surveyed the hat-lined shelves in her chiffonier. *I'll wear one and take one,* she decided. Carefully, she placed her best Sunday bonnet in a round flowered box and selected a green velvet hat, decorated with an ostrich feather, for her journey.

At the doorway, she cast one last look around her childhood room. Tears pricked her brown eyes as she scanned the red velvet window seat and morning chair and realized she'd never again lounge there, reading romantic stories and the engrossing, melancholy tales of Dickens.

She grasped the thick glass doorknob and closed the door behind her, shutting out the sights of her past. She couldn't bear to look at her grandmother's four-poster bed again. Drewry had been born in that bed and, all her life, she'd expected that the fine old piece of furniture would someday serve as her own marriage bed.

A sob escaped her throat. As the years of taking care of Uncle James stretched out, her girlhood friends had married, one by one, and had left Freetown. With each passing year,

Drewry's hope for her own nuptials had diminished, growing dimmer and dimmer like a fading star until, even with a spyglass, a person couldn't see it at all.

❧

"Whoa! Steady there, boy!"

Old Jeb's voice soothed the black stallion, who, unaccustomed to pulling the carriage in the middle of the night, had been spooked by a rabbit darting across the road.

"Only another five mile or so, Miss Drew." Jeb turned to his companion in the driving seat and smiled. "We gonna miss you 'round here, Missy an' me. Not that we don't understand why you gotta go . . ."

Drewry laid her hand on his forearm. "What would I do without you, old friend?" Suddenly, she felt a tear slide down her cheek. "Oh, Jeb, what if I never see you again?"

"I'll be 'round, Miss Drew. Folks like you and me, we's got a bond . . . *here.*" He tapped his thin chest. "So for a while, we'll jus' have to write one 'nother." The old man paused. "It be thanks to your fam'ly that Ol' Jeb know how to write at all. Why, if your daddy hadn't taught me, I'd be jus' as ignorant as them other ex-slaves."

Drewry smiled. "Why, he *had* to teach you to read and write, Jeb. It wasn't right for you to be deprived of the joy of reading the Word of the Lord for yourself."

"Yep." He drew himself up proudly beside her. "Now I reads two chapters from the Good Book each and every day. One from the Old Test-a-ment and one from the New. One thing I do know—" he grew serious, turning to regard her solemnly—"you is in the Lord's hands, Miss Drewry. He ain't about to cast off one o' His own. He got plans for you."

Drewry sighed. She wished her faith were as strong as Jeb's. But rather than admit how long it had been since she'd trusted in God's care, she stiffened her back and folded her hands over the green velvet purse on her lap.

"You'll have to be careful, Jeb, to see that Uncle James doesn't find my letters. I don't want him to know where I am," she said, eager to steer the conversation away from herself.

"Don't you worry none," said Jeb as he slapped the reins against the black horse's back. "I be the one to collect the mail in town. Mr. James ain't done that chore for years." Jeb chuckled softly. "Ain't done none o' the other chores, neither."

Drewry nodded. She knew only too well that Jeb had carried the lion's share of running Plumtree Orchards. Silence fell over them for the duration of their trip south from Freetown to Baltimore.

Jeb didn't speak again until she'd bought her ticket and settled herself on a bench to wait for the early morning train. "Good-bye, Miss Drew," he said, his voice low and gravelly.

Drewry could see tears in the tired old eyes. She reached out and hugged him, an action that earned her a disapproving look from the clerk behind the counter. "Good-bye, Jeb. Take care."

"I'll be prayin' for you, miss. The Lord—He gonna take care of you real good. I knows it."

"Thank you, Jeb," she answered softly. *I only wish I could believe that . . .*

It was a sad moment when he left the train station. Drewry sat near the window in the drafty waiting room and peered through the lumpy glass until Jeb's gentle whip prodded the fine black stallion into action. Then she watched as Jeb, sitting tall and proud in the driver's seat, disappeared into the darkness.

The night was dark as pitch and a moaning wind sighed through the trees. Drewry shivered, though it had been an unseasonably warm night. *The Lord—He gonna take care of you real good. I knows it.* Drewry repeated Jeb's departing words in her mind, vainly trying to draw some small measure of comfort from them. Suddenly, by the light of the flickering oil lamp, she caught her own reflection in the window.

Who was that worried-looking old woman? Where had her belle-of-the-ball, peaches-and-cream complexion gone? Drewry's eyes, as brown as mahogany, looked as bleary and bloodshot as Old Jeb's; her full, crimson mouth pale and drawn; and more than a few strands of her dark hair had escaped from the two braids piled on top of her head.

Oh, but you're going to have to do better than this, she chided herself, covering her unkempt hair with her hat. *You may be down, Drewry Sheffield, but you're not finished. Not by a long shot. So you were gambled away by your only living relative. You've still got your health, your youth, and enough money to start a new life.*

And where there's life, there's hope . . .

two

It had been the longest, loneliest night of Drewry's life. Sitting upright on the hard, wooden bench at Baltimore's train station, she clutched her one-way ticket like a life preserver. She'd plunked down enough money to take her from Baltimore to Florida, if she chose to go that far. She had never been farther from home than Baltimore, and the world seemed as foreboding as it had all those years ago in Joshua Taylor's law office.

From time to time, Drewry's head bobbed as she stole a moment of much-needed slumber. But each time she dozed off, she snapped awake, blinked, and shook off the drowsy feelings. *Can't sleep now,* she told herself. *Not here with these carpetbaggers milling about . . .*

She heard the mournful whistle of her escape vehicle as it chugged down the tracks, and half-carried, half-dragged her overstuffed valise and lone hatbox onto the boarding platform, the heels of her black boots clicking on the polished marble floors. Fear and excitement knotted her stomach as she stood, alone among the crowd of prospective passengers, waiting for the big, black engine to grind to a steaming halt.

"This train's goin' south," the conductor called, leaping from the first passenger car. "Those goin' south . . . all abo-o-oard!" He stood beside the bottom step, hand extended palm up, to accept tickets.

"'Mornin'," he said, nodding as passengers boarded the train. "Watch your step now."

Drewry placed her bag alongside others that would soon be stowed in the baggage car, and said a brief, silent prayer—in case God was listening, after all—that what she'd packed would arrive safely at her destination. The few essentials she'd stuffed into her suitcase were all she had to call her own now.

"There's a couple of window seats left in the second car," the conductor whispered as she handed him her ticket. "You look like a young lady who wants to see where she's goin'."

She gave him a half-hearted grin. "Thank you, sir." Drewry's voice wavered slightly, and she bit back bitter tears. Thanks to her uncle's latest shenanigans, she had no idea *where* she might be headed, or what might be in store for her once she arrived there.

Some quick ciphering told her that she had enough money to last her six months, seven, if she spent her dollars wisely and lived frugally. When she finally did decide on a place of residence, Drewry would need a job immediately. Trouble was, she had no idea what sort of work a young woman of her station might be qualified to do. She'd helped Jeb run the plantation, keeping the books, and she'd nursed Uncle James back to health. *But who'd pay me to do* those *things?* Drewry wondered.

With one white-gloved hand, she lifted the heavy cotton skirt of her plaid dress and ruffled white petticoats so as not to trip as she climbed the train's three steep steps. For balance, she grasped a thick horizontal brass handrail with the other hand.

Before Drewry knew it, she was walking down the carpeted narrow aisle of the train, pressing the green velvet drawstring of her small purse protectively against her waist. A lady nodded as Drewry passed. A gentleman tipped his hat. Since Drewry wasn't inclined to make friendly conversation at the moment, she walked wordlessly to the far end of the car, nearest the doors that connected it to the next car, and settled into the cushioned window seat against the back wall.

With a sinking heart, she realized she'd packed in such a rush that she didn't have a book or her embroidery or anything else, for that matter, to keep her hands and mind occupied during the trip. Drewry wondered how on earth she'd pass the time as she headed south.

For the time being, she fussed with the folds of her skirts so that its hem rested neatly atop her black-polished high-heeled boots. For an instant, she wondered if she'd remembered to toss her button hook into her valise—getting the high-button boots off and on again would be a chore without it—

"Goodness gracious sakes alive!" said the young woman who stood before her. "I hope I'm around to catch you when you swoon. It's sure to happen, ya know, 'cause all bundled up in those frilly clothes the way you are, you're sure to sweat like a pig."

The blonde flopped in an unladylike heap into the seat across from Drewry's. "I do declare! Don't believe I've ever seen a warmer spring day, have you?" She fanned her face with one, ungloved hand.

Drewry's tight-lipped smile, she hoped, would convey to the girl that she should find another seatmate.

"My, my," the young woman tried again, "you look like you've just swallowed a mouthful of wormy apple!" Giggling, she added, "You're not a day older than me, I'll bet, so why on earth do you look like you've got the weight of Old Father Time on your shoulders?"

With that, she reached out and lightly smacked Drewry's knee. "Smile, for goodness sake! Didn't your mama ever tell you that frownin' makes you old and wrinkly before your time?"

Her mama hadn't taught her much prior to her death, Drewry thought sadly. It had been Missy, Jeb's wife, who had taught her to behave like a proper lady. Still, Drewry couldn't help but return the girl's grin. She extended her gloved hand. "If we're to be traveling companions, I suppose introductions are in order. My name is Drewry Sheffield."

The girl moved Drewry's arm up and down like a pump

handle. "Pleased ta meet ya! I'm Suzie Quantoserra." She leaned forward and whispered loudly, "They call me Suzie Q for short."

"Pleased to meet you, Suzie." Drewry plucked her hand from the girl's tight grasp. "What's your destination?"

Suzie rolled her green eyes heavenward. "Richmond, Virginia," she said, frowning, "where I'll mind a rich old fella's motherless brats." She slumped against the seat back, feigning exhaustion. "I'm supposed to meet them at the Richmond station."

She sighed heavily. "The lady at the employment agency wrote Mr. Fancy Pants that I have *years* of experience rearin' other folks's young'uns." She leaned forward again and whispered conspiratorially, "Truth is, I spent a few months helpin' my sister after she birthed twins." Snickering, Suzie sat back. "What he don't know won't hurt him, right?"

Drewry inhaled sharply. Suzie barely knew her, yet she had just freely admitted that she'd not only lied to the employment agency, but planned to continue the charade when she met her future employer! Having grown up without parents herself, Drewry's heart ached a little for the two motherless children innocently awaiting Suzie's indifferent brand of care.

"Oh, now don't go gettin' all misty-eyed on me," Suzie said, as though she could read Drewry's mind. "Why, those folks have got so much money, they could burn it all winter to keep warm and still not use it all up, I'll bet! Never any need to pity the rich, I always say."

"But, Suzie, those children have no mother . . ."

Suzie rolled her eyes again. "Really, now, you can't be serious. What a mama can't give 'em, their money kin buy."

Drewry blinked once before replying, her voice soft and husky, "No amount of money can buy them what they need most . . . *love.*"

Without a moment's hesitation, Suzie waved the idea away.

"Tish tosh, all those young'uns want is somebody to wait on 'em hand and foot. Well, I'll see to it they don't go 'round thinkin' they're better than others, just on accounta they got more dollars in the bank than most folks. 'Spare the rod and spoil the child,' the Bible says." The happy light that had glowed in Suzie's eyes burned hot and angry now.

"You can teach them far more with love and kindness than you can with harsh words and spankings," Drewry snapped, a little angry herself.

"Hoo-boy! So, Miss Frilly Duds has a temper, has she?" Laughing, Suzie smacked Drewry on the knee again. "Don't get all lathered up now, sweetie. I was just funnin' with you. I ain't gonna waste any of my energy on those brats, I can promise you that! I'll do exactly what Mr. Fancy Pants tells me to, and not one whit more." She jerked her head emphatically.

Just then the conductor sang out, "All abo-o-ard that's goin' aboard!"

A moment later, the hissing, chugging train lurched forward. Steam rose from the engine and floated back over the cars that trailed behind it, temporarily fogging Drewry's vision of the platform. Suddenly, she desperately needed a last look at the Baltimore station, at the tall, gray-walled building and the narrow walkway where Jeb had said his final goodbye. At the road alongside it that had carried him out of her life, perhaps forever. At the streets and buildings where she'd followed her parents—and her Uncle James in happier days—to carry on the family business.

But by the time the smoke cleared, the station was out of sight. Hot, bitter tears stung Drewry's eyes. Very likely, she'd never see this town again. Not if marriage to Porter Hopkins came with the trip home!

ঙ

My, but she was tired. So very tired. Drewry kept her eyes closed until she felt certain they'd left Baltimore—and its memories—behind. Only then did she open them to peer through the window at the rolling hills of Maryland's farmland.

"This seat taken?"

Drewry glanced away from the passing landscape and in the direction of the masculine voice. A soldier, standing at attention, stood in the aisle, his slanting blue eyes fused to Suzie's flirty green ones.

The girl slid nearer the window and patted the empty space beside her. "Set yourself down, why don't ya, and take a load off?"

Grinning, he removed his navy blue cap and sat down beside Suzie. "Name's Williams," he said, his right hand forming a proper salute. "Sergeant Duke Williams."

Drewry needn't have worried what she'd do to pass the time between Baltimore and her new mystery home. For the next hour, Suzie and Duke chattered like a couple of chipmunks.

As they talked, absorbed in one another, her mind wandered, from thoughts of her happy childhood with Uncle James—before the War—to thoughts of the hard work and long hours it had taken to keep the plantation running in his absence.

She hadn't minded adding "nurse" to her long list of daily duties when he came home from battle, scarred in body, mind, and soul. At first, the prayers she had prayed beside his sickbed were for his survival. When it became evident that he would live, she beseeched God to help her uncle accept his fate. The left side of his handsome face had been terribly scarred by shrapnel, his left eye forever blinded by a chip of the metal, and half of his left foot had been blown away by a cannonball.

Self-pity was an ugly thing, Drewry realized as she watched her once-lively uncle descend deeper and deeper into the dark abyss of despair. "It's not that I'm vain," he told her once, holding her hand tight as he waited for the whiskey, prescribed as pain medication by the doctor, to take effect. "But Drew-girl . . . how will I get by? How will I live my life, now that I'm no longer a whole man?"

She'd tried to explain that he was the same man . . . inside. But he hadn't been convinced.

"Because of me, dozens of young men are dead," he said, bitter tears punctuating his confession. "I sent them to their deaths. I never deserved more brass buttons on my uniform than they had . . . I didn't deserve to survive . . ."

Her prayers, by this time, had changed completely in tone and intent, for as the days passed and his physical pain decreased, her uncle's mental anguish increased, and Drewry began to lose hope.

James fashioned himself a gnarled cane. It seemed that with each painful, halting step, his inner turmoil grew. Her prayers now were simply that he'd reach inside himself and find some courage, some semblance of the man he used to be. Drewry missed his sweet smile. His teasing jibes. His hearty laughter and his zest for life. She missed his bear hugs. The way he whistled as he moved about the house and grounds. The way he hummed as he trimmed his neat, dark beard every morning. She missed the mischievous gleam in his crisp, blue eyes, and the quirky smirk that slanted his mustachioed mouth. She missed being able to count on him to be there for her, to protect and care for her, as he'd promised all those years ago in Joshua Taylor's richly-appointed office. Most of all, she missed believing in her Uncle James's unconditional, unstoppable love. It seemed the harder she prayed, however, the worse James behaved.

Drewry wasn't a helpless child any longer; she was a young woman when he returned—tattered, torn, and battle-weary—from the Civil War. In the years since, self-pity had quickly turned to self-blame, and then to self-loathing. In fact, he seemed to find peace only when basking in the golden glow of whiskey.

He gambled. And cursed. And spent money like water. This once kind-hearted man now thought nothing of slapping employees about and yelling the most hurtful epithets at his business associates. And though he'd never actually carried out a threat, he'd even taken to intimidating Drewry with physical violence.

Stubbornly, she clung to the hope that, if she believed strongly enough, the man her uncle had been before the War would come back to her. She dared not send such thoughts heavenward any longer, however, for Drewry had thoroughly convinced herself she wasn't worthy of God's ear. For not one prayer she'd ever prayed had been answered.

Instead, she had gone about doing all that was humanly possible to make her beloved uncle comfortable, though he usually fought her every step of the way.

She had withstood his hateful words. Cried herself to sleep too many nights to count, grieving for the loss of yet another loved one (for Uncle James, as she'd known him, was certainly gone). She'd never felt more alone, more abandoned. This latest fiasco, she believed, proved that she had lost him for good. How else could she explain that he'd so easily agreed to hand her over, like common chattel, to the likes of Porter Hopkins?

This abandonment hurt worse than any that had come before it, for it reminded Drewry how worthless her life must be, how unlovable, if even her beloved Uncle James could treat her so casually.

A sudden flurry of activity roused Drewry from her melancholy thoughts. "We're off to the dining car," Suzie announced, clinging possessively to Duke's arm. "Wipe that mournful look off your face, and maybe we'll let ya come with us!" She looked to her companion for approval.

With a quick nod and a friendly grin, Duke added, "We'd be honored if you'd join us, Miss Drewry."

I shouldn't, she told herself. *But I am hungry . . .* If she didn't go with them now, she'd have to eat alone later. And since she'd probably be spending countless hours alone in whatever town she decided to make her new home, Drewry decided she'd best take advantage of what might well be the last offer of friendship she'd hear in a long, long time.

She rose slowly and gave as much of a curtsy as the tight space would allow. "Thank you for inviting me," she said quietly.

"Oh, it wasn't nothin'," Suzie said, waving away Drewry's gratitude. "Just don't spill anything and embarrass me," she said, giggling over her shoulder as she led the way down the narrow aisle.

Drewry followed the couple. *She's right. You'd* better *take care not to spill anything,* she told herself, *because there aren't many things to wear in place of this dress if you do!*

&

Drewry returned to her seat long before Duke and Suzie, feeling the couple wanted a few minutes alone before Suzie was to disembark in Richmond. Drewry stared at the changing scenery, amazed that the weather could so effectively mirror her mood. A steady, unrelenting rain pelted the glass, each drop sliding to the windowsill before disappearing. Thunder rolled and lightning sliced the slate-colored sky as Drewry's spirits continued to fall.

Suzie wouldn't get much of a welcome in Richmond, Drewry realized, if the storm didn't let up. But then, she didn't deserve much of a welcome, considering what she intended for the unsuspecting young widower and his innocent, motherless children.

The girl was six, Suzie had said, and the boy just three. Their mother, the agency had told Suzie, had died giving birth to the boy. Mr. Fancy Pants, as Suzie insisted on calling him, had tried to be both mother and father to his children, and had

succeeded through that first year. Now his housekeeper was
growing older and his farm was getting bigger, and he simply
couldn't continue as before. Drewry felt a pang of pity for
him, whoever he might be. Surely he'd be sorely disappointed
in the flighty young girl the employment agency was sending
him to care for his children.

Suzie, Drewry decided, was an odd blend of silly and smart.
"Crazy like a fox," Jeb would have said if he'd met the brassy
young woman. She was wearing a blue satin dress with a low-
cut bodice—totally inappropriate for day wear and completely
wrong for traveling, Drewry thought disapprovingly. Nor was
Suzie wearing gloves or a hat. Her loud, brash voice was further proof that the girl hadn't been properly schooled in ladylike deportment.

During dinner in the dining car, Suzie's table manners had
been atrocious. When Drewry pointed out the polished brass
lantern on the starched white tablecloth, Suzie merely stared
at her reflection in it and fluffed her blond curls. And when
Drewry commented on the velvet draperies, tied back with thick,
gold-tasseled cords and extending from ceiling to floor, Suzie
reached out and stuck her fingers into the thick, soft folds . . .
leaving a buttery stain behind!

"Next stop, Richmond," the conductor announced, interrupting Drewry's musings.

"Excuse me, sir," Drewry said. "Would you happen to have
the time?"

The lanky man pulled a gold watch from his pocket and
popped open its lid. "Fifteen minutes before one o'clock," he
said before snapping it shut again. "Somebody meetin' you in
Richmond?"

Drewry shook her head. "I'm not getting off at this stop.
Only my seatmate . . ."

"Then would you like me to hunt you up a pillow? Looks
like you could use some sleep."

Drewry smiled at him. "No. Thank you just the same."

The conductor nodded and tipped his hat, then disappeared into the next car. In a moment, the train ground to a halt.

Drewry stared out the window at the expectant faces of the people on the platform. Among the dozens of individuals, all scanning the windows for a glimpse of their relatives and friends, one small group stood out: A tall, well-built man with a big, black umbrella was holding tight to a small boy. The man leaned forward, as if checking to make sure the boy still grasped the little girl's hand. Then, satisfied, it seemed, with what he saw, he straightened again and watched as the passengers disembarked.

Suzie and Duke returned just then. "Oh, goodness gracious me!" Suzie exclaimed, peering out the window. "If it isn't Mr. Fancy Pants!"

"How can you be so sure?" Drewry asked, since the girl had never met him.

"The lady at the agency said he'd be wearing a blue silk tie, so's I'd know him when I blew into town."

Drewry glanced back at the platform. The man did, indeed, have a blue tie knotted at his throat.

"I sure hope this rain lets up," Suzie said, "'cause I'd hate to leave 'em standin' there, gettin' all wet . . ."

Drewry smiled. "They'll only be out there a moment more. Once the porter finds your bags, you'll all be on your way."

Suzie giggled and snuggled closer to Duke. "We—ll . . . we have a little announcement to make, don't we, honey?" she said, kissing the soldier's cheek. "We're getting off in Richmond, all right, but only long enough to find a preacher!"

"A preacher!" Drewry's brown eyes widened in disbelief. "You don't mean to say that in the little while I was gone . . ."

Suzie beamed. "Yes, indeedy. We've discovered we have a lot in common, and Duke here has asked me to be his bride!"

Duke smiled shyly. "And lucky me . . . she said yes."

Drewry couldn't believe her ears. How could anyone come to such an important decision so quickly? "But—but what about . . .?"

"Mr. Fancy Pants?" Suzie supplied. "Oh, tish tosh, he'll be just fine. He'll write a few more letters, and before you know it, he'll have another slave girl lined up to watch over his brats." She shrugged unconcernedly.

Drewry looked at the man again. At the expectant expression on his face. At the stiff way he held his broad shoulders. At the worry lines creasing his handsome brow. "You can't just leave him there, waiting . . . with no explanation . . ."

"Just watch me!"

With that, the couple headed down the steps, and arm-in-arm, they faced the train. When Suzie spied Drewry's face in the window, she grinned and waved. "Bye-bye," she mouthed through the glass.

Suddenly, Drewry had an idea. She *could* get off in Richmond, after all. She could walk right up to Mr. Fancy Pants and introduce herself as the nanny he'd sent for. The agency hadn't given him a description, Suzie had explained, so he wouldn't know . . .

Drewry had never done a dishonest thing in all her life, but then, never in all her life had she been in a situation like this one. Right now, this little deception seemed a justifiable— even necessary—means to an end. Uncle James had sold her to Porter Hopkins to secure his future of drinking and gambling, and no doubt her uncle—or worse, Porter Hopkins himself—would come looking for her. Surely, though, he'd never think to search for her on a southern plantation—in the position of a nanny!

In Drewry's mind, it was the perfect solution to both her problem *and* that poor man's. And it wasn't as though she'd mislead him about *everything*—only about the fact that an employment agency had sent her to Richmond to look after his children.

She *would* look after them—far better than Suzie had planned to. The sight of the children tugged at her heart. How well she knew the pain of growing up without a mama!

Telling such an outrageous lie tormented her conscience like a hair shirt. But it did seem to present a workable solution . . . Making her decision, Drewry gathered up her skirts and hurried from the train. As she stepped down onto the platform, she said a quick prayer of thanks that the rain had let up, leaving out her confession of wrongdoing. She'd tend to that later.

As her eyes met his, Drewry's stomach lurched. *This lie would certainly be easier to tell if the man were fat and bald,* she told herself. *How will you look into that handsome face and . . .*

Just then, he waved. She nodded to acknowledge his greeting, then stepped over briskly to join the little family.

"Chase Auburn," he said, smiling and extending the hand that had, until moments before, held his little boy's. "And you must be our new nanny."

Her hand trembled as she placed it tentatively into his. "Drewry," she said matter-of-factly. "Drewry Sheffield."

"This is Sam," Chase said, patting his son's dark head. Then ruffling his daughter's blond curls, he continued the introductions. "And this is Sally. Say hello to Miss Sheffield, children."

"Hello, Miss Sheffield," the little boy parroted, clinging to his father's arm.

"Hello, Miss Sheffield," the little girl echoed, taking a step closer to her father's side.

Drewry's heart melted. In the wide-eyed gazes, she could read their fear and uncertainty. Who was this stranger who would be assuming control of their young lives? Suddenly, the lie was the last thing on Drewry's mind. She simply wanted to reassure these frightened little ones.

Stooping to make herself child-sized, Drewry took each of their hands in her own and smiled warmly. "Sam and Sally, what lovely children you are."

"Thank you, Miss Sheffield," they said in unison.

Drewry laughed softly. "Would you mind very much calling me Drewry? 'Miss Sheffield' is quite a mouthful."

They looked to their father. At his approving nod, they grinned. "Doo-ree," said little Sam.

It warmed Drewry's heart to see the fear fade from their eyes. Gently, she squeezed their little hands. "I'll take good care of you," she said. "I promise."

three

Chase Auburn had not expected such a comely woman to arrive to serve as his children's nanny. Actually, when he thought of it, the word *beautiful* was a more fitting description of Miss Drewry Sheffield. Slight of build, the top of her head barely reached his shoulder, despite being piled high with thick dark curls. Her skin was the color of milk, and those eyes—wide and longer-lashed than a a doe's, though travel-weary—spoke of her intelligence. Yet, looking into those sad brown eyes, he sensed something more.

But *what* sadness could be burdening such a handsome young woman?

Neither had he expected the Baltimore employment agency to send someone whose clothing and mannerisms told of a background of elegance and refinement. Just what kind of girls were taking to nannying children these days? Well, he reminded himself, since the War, many a family fortune had been lost. Surely that fact alone made it necessary for some young ladies of good breeding to find ways to earn their own money. But rather than ask potentially distressing questions, Chase concentrated on making the lady nanny feel welcome, especially now that advancing age had made the daily care of small children a painful exercise for Matilda.

On their way to the carriage, he quietly observed as the new nanny chatted with Sam and Sally. She commented on Sally's rag doll, saying that she'd had one very much like it as a child. She asked Sam if he knew his letters yet. Under Miss Sheffield's tender attention, the children's faces seemed to blossom—almost magically—like two upturned sunflowers. Amazingly, although his children had always been shy and reserved around strangers, each now had a firm grip on one of her hands.

Chase dug his own hands deep into the pockets of his coat and touched the small ferrotype of Theresa he always carried. Deprived of their own mother, the children craved a motherly presence. Assured by the comfortable chatter between Miss Sheffield, Sam, and Sally, Chase sighed and offered a silent prayer of thanks. He'd had his doubts about sending for a nanny, sight unseen, but he'd trusted his heavenly Father to provide the perfect one for his family.

"You must be tired, Miss Sheffield," he said as he took Drewry's white-gloved hand and helped her into the carriage. He caught the distinctly feminine fragrance of lavender and smiled. "Please make yourself comfortable. We should reach Magnolia Grange in just over an hour."

Seconds later, a black porter loaded her bulging valise and hatbox into the luggage compartment at the rear of the carriage. Chase tipped him handsomely.

"Thank you, Mistah Auburn, suh. But that be too much money."

"Not at all, Patrick. 'The workman is worthy of his hire,' remember?"

The young man beamed gratefully. "Yes, suh. G'day, suh." He inclined his head respectfully and strode back to the train.

"Before the war, Patrick was a slave on a neighboring plantation," Chase explained as Drewry tidied her skirt and loosened the green velvet bow of her hat. "He was a beaten man back then. Now look at him! Dignity and self-respect are powerful forces."

"Yes, indeed," said Drewry, flashing a smile that warmed his lonely soul like sunshine melting ice on a pond. He didn't know why her approval should evoke such a curious feeling of pleasure, but a tremor of excitement coursed through his blood, even if tinged with guilt.

In fact, the young woman's sweet smile put a spring into Chase's step as he climbed into the driver's seat and gathered the reins into his leather-gloved hands. Her delicate scent, the light touch of her hand, the gentle tone of her voice filled his senses. He knew, of course, that forever mourning his beloved Theresa wouldn't bring her back, but was it right to take such pleasure in the company of another woman? Desperate to shake the forbidden images, he slapped the reins across the backs of his pair of roan stallions.

Well, at least his children were more content that they had been since the Lord called his wife home, Chase thought as he listened to the hum of their voices. And as the horses' hooves clattered along the cobblestone streets of Richmond, he consciously turned his heart to prayer, echoing Job's words: *"The Lord giveth and the Lord taketh away. Blessed be the name of the Lord."*

❧

Drewry remembered riding in a buckboard when, as a small girl, she had accompanied Jeb to Fells Point for supplies. Many times, she had ridden in her father's surrey, a fancy, gold-fringed affair with a high, bouncing seat and big metal wheels. But never in her life had she been conveyed in a carriage so grand as Chase Auburn's.

The entire chassis, jet black and gleaming, was richly trimmed in the same polished brass that adorned the two beveled-glass lanterns mounted up front. Hand-turned wheels with gently tapered spokes were secured by bright red cotters. Drewry couldn't be sure if the ride felt smooth because of the great size of the wheels or because of the springs that allowed the buggy itself to bounce ever so gently with every *clip clop* of the horses' hooves.

Red leather seats, tufted and overstuffed, reminded her of the thick feather mattress on her bed at home. *If this is any indication of what I'll see when I arrive at Magnolia Grange,*

Drewry thought, *my new home will be quite grand indeed!*

She looked down at the children, snuggled up to her on either side. Her heart ached for them. Growing up without a mother gave her great compassion for them. With a sigh, she remembered the pain of losing her own parents.

In those first, lonely years after their deaths and before the War had taken her Uncle James away from her, Drewry had blossomed under his loving ministrations. And old Jeb's wife, Missy, despite having been born into slavery, knew what was required of a proper lady, and had taught Drewry to conduct herself with grace and dignity.

It was at Missy's knee that Drewry had learned to sew and crochet and embroider. It had been Missy's hands that had guided hers on the ivory keys of her mother's baby grand. It was Jeb who had taught Drewry the soft, soulful melodies that soothed many a sad moment, and Jeb whose gentle advice explained away unkind words and deeds. Drewry decided right then and there that these babes would receive the best of everything she had learned from Uncle James, Jeb, and Missy.

Her heart ached for Chase, too. The death of his wife must have cost him a huge chunk of his heart. Oh, he smiled a wide, friendly grin, all right, but Drewry noticed that his smile never quite managed to reach those dark brown eyes. She likened his grief to the way she had felt when Uncle James returned from his final battle, changed—overnight, it seemed—from the loving man he had been.

Surely, each and every time he looked into the eyes of his children, Chase was reminded of his wife. Drewry prayed for the strength to help ease his burdens, as well as to be a good nanny to his children. Because, if the truth be told, she liked Chase Auburn. Liked him a bit too much, perhaps, considering they'd only just met.

She sensed great strength in this man. Yes, he was tall and powerfully built and could no doubt heft a hundred-pound sack with ease. But it was strength of character that ebbed from every pore, and that kind of strength, she knew, had to be rooted deep in a person's soul.

Halfway through the ride from Richmond's rail station to the plantation, the children fell asleep. Drewry closed her own eyes, so that she could picture their father in the privacy of her imagination.

Chase was a striking man, by anyone's standards. Tall and well-muscled, his broad shoulders and narrow waist proclaimed his masculinity. Still, it was his face that intrigued her most. Dark brows arched above near-black eyes, and when he looked at her with that penetrating gaze, it seemed he could see all the way into her very heart. His easy grin revealed even, white teeth.

Drewry's thoughts circled round and round the handsome man who would be her employer. What were the chances, she wondered, that someday he would be more? What would it feel like to be encircled by those powerful arms? And how would her lips respond to a soft, sweet kiss from those well-shaped lips?

Suddenly Drewy's eyes opened wide. *The very idea!* she scolded herself. *You're a hired hand. An employee, and nothing more. And, what's worse, you're here under false pretenses! Get those silly, romantic notions right out of your head, or you're sure to bungle this job even before you begin it!*

Drewry couldn't seriously entertain thoughts of a romance with a man like Chase Auburn. She was obviously unworthy of love. *Why would a man like that want you, Drewry Sheffield, a girl whose only relative thought so little of her that he gambled her away like a meaningless possession? A girl too unworthy even to have her prayers answered?*

It wasn't that Drewry was angry with God for His silence. At least, not anymore. With each passing year, although she continued to pray for the things she needed, as her dear mother had taught her, her faith died a bit every time those prayers went unanswered. Gradually, she learned to get by without seeking God's help. Her present situation was only further evidence that He wasn't about to rescue her from any ordeal, no matter how terrifying—not even marriage to the vile and despicable Porter Hopkins.

As recently as last night, she'd prayed that something—someone—would put a stop to Uncle James's horrible plan. But she'd been forced to escape by her own hand. Jeb had helped out, of course. But that didn't count. He was *always* helping out. So here she sat, with only a few hundred dollars to her name, one valise and a lone hatbox to call her own, traveling to a strange new place she'd have to learn to call home . . .

Suddenly Chase shouted back to her from the driver's seat. "Look, Miss Sheffield, we're nearly home!" No amount of description could have prepared Drewry for her first view of the plantation. "Our land begins here," said Chase over his shoulder.

Following the inclination of his head, she saw the neat, board fence that outlined the north edge of his property. He gestured eastward, toward the hilly horizon, using his whip handle as a pointer. "See that line of poplars over there?"

Drewry hugged her tiny purse tightly, knowing that even before he spoke the words, Chase would tell her that Magnolia Grange's eastern boundary went as far as the eye could see.

She wondered how many acres made up the grand plantation. Hundreds, maybe even thousands. Drewry sighed and glanced at Sally and Sam. With such a large spread to oversee, Chase could be gone for days at a time, and she'd be alone with his children. It was an awesome responsibility, and Drewry silently promised she'd never let him down.

She turned to peer through the oval glass window in the back of the carriage. Then, facing forward again, she stifled a

of the embrace knocked her hat right off.

"Miss Sheffield, may I introduce my housekeeper, Matilda," announced Chase as he stooped to retrieve the wisp of millinery from the white marble floor.

"P—Pleased to meet you, Matilda," Drewry sputtered when finally released from the she-bear hug.

"Matilda used to be my nanny when I was a lad in knickers," said Chase, grinning. "That's why I'm spoiled rotten, isn't it, Matilda?"

"The world be hard enough on chil'rens," answered Matilda gravely, as she straightened to her full, towering height. "So I says spoil 'em whilst you can. Ain't that right, Miss Drewry?"

"If by spoiling, you mean giving them all the love their little hearts can hold, I agree," Drewry replied, casting a quick look at Sam and Sally, who were doing their best to suppress a giggle.

"I can tell we is gonna git along fine, Miss Drewry," proclaimed Matilda. "We both got a mama's heart, jus' like the Good Lord's, ain't that right, Mr. Chase?"

The tall man stood bemused, still holding Drewry's hat. "No truer words were ever spoken." He nodded solemnly, then flashed Drewry a dazzling smile.

"Miss Sheffield, may I introduce the other members of our household." Chase nodded toward a lithe young girl whose face was surrounded by a mass of fiery curls. "This is Bridget McKenna, our serving girl. Bridget came to us all the way from Cork, Ireland."

Drewry stepped forward and took the girl's hand, surprised by the strength in the slender fingers. "How very nice to meet you, Bridget."

"And this is our faithful Simon," said Chase, indicating a lean older black man. "He helps Matilda take care of the house."

Simon inclined his head respectfully. His build and demeanor reminded her of Jeb.

"And last but certainly not least, our foreman, Claib. He's the reason we have poinsettias at Christmas, roses at Easter, and orchids all year round. And without him, my crop and hothouse experiments would surely have failed—as predicted loudly and often by our tobacco- and cotton-farming neighbors."

Claib, a brawny man with skin the color of coal, fingered the stained hat in his huge leathery hands and tipped his head politely. "Miss Sheffield, I hopes you be happy here. We's right glad to have you."

"Please, all of you, call me Drewry," she said, beaming around the small circle. "You've made me feel right at home."

Suddenly she felt a tug on her skirt. Sally looked up at her pleadingly. "Miss Sheffield . . . I mean Drewry . . . Sam and me want you to be happy so you'll stay with us forever."

Drewry bit her lip to halt the tears that threatened, then knelt and hugged the child, smoothing the tousled locks. "Of course, I'll stay, darling!" she cried . . . *or at least until someone catches on to my bluff,* she thought.

Chase, she noticed, had been watching her carefully. No doubt he would soon be contacting the Baltimore employment agency to assure them of the nanny's safe arrival. Then, when they responded to his letter, they'd surely tell him she wasn't the young woman they had sent!

Still, there was much more at stake now than her own safety. Chase's children were vulnerable. Needy. Everything they did and said cried out for a mother's affections. What if several months passed before Chase learned the truth about her . . . ? Her thoughts were interrupted by an announcement from Matilda.

"Dinner's 'mos' ready. Will an hour be 'nough time to freshen up?"

"More than enough," Drewry assured her. "But someone will have to tell me where—" She cast an inquiring glance in

Chase's direction.

He nodded and led the way up a magnificent walnut-railed staircase. Claib trailed behind Drewry and the children, carrying her valise and hatbox.

"Anyone living in this house who doesn't feel loved and welcome . . . well, it's not Matilda's fault," Chase called over his shoulder.

His remark, intended kindly, she knew, struck Drewry's heart like a blade of cold steel. Yes, Matilda and the others had made her feel a part of the family right away. And the children had certainly welcomed her warmly. But what would happen if they learned that she had deliberately deceived them? What if someone called her bluff?

Who would love her then?

four

"Oh, my!" Upon entering the dining room of Magnolia Grange, Drewry caught her breath, stunned by the splendor of her sur-roundings.

A six-candle ormolu chandelier cast soft shadows along the red velvet fleur-de-lis wallpaper, highlighted the golden oak sideboard, and glinted off the silver tea service and blue Delft china. The scent of fresh flowers permeated the room.

"Come in!" Chase Auburn, dapper in his black evening coat, strode across the hardwood floor to take her hand.

A feeling of pleasure coursed through Drewry at his touch and she found herself blushing. "Thank you, Mr. Auburn."

"Please . . . call me Chase." He eyed her meaningfully, nod-ding toward the children. "We'll be a team, you know."

He led her to the table and pulled out the heavy, leather-backed chair. "I hope you don't mind, but I've asked my other . . . helpers . . . to join us tonight in a special meal to welcome you."

Drewry lifted her gaze to meet his. His dark eyes radiated a warmth that made her heart beat faster. *Perhaps I've found a home here, safe from Uncle James,* she thought. *If only . . . if only I can keep my secret.*

She smoothed the lace trim of her blue calico dress, grateful that she hadn't had room to pack her fancier gowns or her six-hooped petticoats; two hoops were plenty for a nanny. Ner-vously she brushed back the wide, sausage curls that cascaded down her back, hoping Chase wouldn't think her a silly fol-lower of the latest trends in Godey's fashion plates.

"Of course I don't mind," she said. "I'm a servant, too."

"And I, also."

Drewry shot him a puzzled look.

"We are all servants of Christ here," he explained softly.

She nodded, her flush deepening. But Drewry found it comforting that Chase was a man who lived by his convictions. Perhaps he would find it in his heart to forgive her if . . . Quickly, she cast aside the possibility of being exposed as the impostor she was.

At that moment Matilda brought in a steaming soup tureen. Sally and Sam, dressed in their best, sat swinging their legs impatiently. Claib and Simon were seated side by side, fidgeting a little, as if somewhat unsure of themselves. Bridget, her flaming mane caught up in a black velvet band, helped Matilda serve the meal.

Inhaling the savory aromas of clam chowder, roast chicken with sage dressing, creamed sweet corn and green peas, and steamed Indian pudding, Drewry suddenly realized how hungry she was.

"Shall we bow our heads for grace?" As the little group complied, Chase began, "Heavenly Father, bless us, we beseech Thee, and bless this food. We thank Thee for finding it in Thy will to bring Miss Sheffield to us, for making her part of our famil. . . ."

Drewry's heart lifted. So Chase *was* happy to have her at Magnolia Grange! He continued to pray, asking the Lord's blessing on the crops. The humble prayer of this strong man of faith touched her deeply. He spoke quietly, but with an assurance that he was addressing the God of the universe and that He was listening to every word.

Drewry longed to feel such confidence in God again. To believe that He would hear her prayers. To know that He would not reject or abandon her . . . as her own flesh and blood had done . . .

"For all these things, we thank Thee, Father, in the name of our Lord Jesus Christ, amen," Chase finished.

Looking up, Drewry found his eyes on her. Quickly, she pretended to be absorbed in undoing her napkin. Even the silver napkin ring told her she had been accepted into Chase's family. A well-bred family presented a guest with a cleverly folded napkin, while napkin rings were reserved for family.

Family, she mused. *But what if they find out I'm not who they think I am?* Glumly she placed the linen square over her lap.

"Drewry, may I offer you some beverage?" With a silver pitcher poised over her cut-glass goblet, Chase quirked his brow. "The good Dr. Hires, inventor of root beer, claims it is one of the best blood purifiers in the world. Says it imparts strength and a clear complexion."

Laughing softly, she held up her glass. "How can I refuse our national temperance drink?"

"It's a favorite in this house," said Chase as he filled Drewry's glass and began filling Sally's. "But, Miss Sheffield, I must warn you that the food here may not be as rich as you prefer."

"Oh?" Drewry eyed the fare. Now that he mentioned it, she did notice an absence of the rich, creamy sauces that graced many tables of means.

"Yes, our Matilda is a devotee of Miss Catharine Beecher's cooking reforms."

"The sister of authoress Harriet Beecher Stowe?" Drewry asked as she took a sip of the cool, sweet root beer.

"The same. Why, her reforms are making as big a stir on gastronomy as *Uncle Tom's Cabin* made in the world of literature."

"What does Miss Beecher recommend?" asked Drewry as she accepted a chowder-filled bowl from Matilda.

"To eat more simply—less flesh, more vegetables. She herself eats no meat. She claims in her books that this diet will prevent the harmful effects of rich foods on the digestion—

namely, dyspepsia."

Drewry felt her cheeks redden once more. Speaking of one's internal organs in mixed company was decidedly embarrassing.

Chase seemed to sense her discomfort. "Please forgive me. I quite forgot my manners," he said, his dark eyes concerned. "I'd better watch my tongue, or Matilda will fetch her switch."

"Yessuh!" retorted Matilda from the far end of the table, partly obscured from Drewry's vision by the rising steam from the tureen. "Miss Sheffield be a lady, plain as day."

"Ah, yes," Chase agreed, slanting Drewry an appraising glance. "It's quite plain, indeed. Tell us, Miss Sheffield, about your home, your people."

She put down her spoon and cast about for an explanation that would protect her identity, while at the same time, would not be an outright lie. "I grew up on a fruit plantation in northern Maryland," she began hesitantly. "My parents were both killed when I was about Sally's age. After that, my Uncle James raised me. Then the War came along and . . ." Her voice trailed away on a little catch.

"There, there," Chase broke in. "No need to go into the painful details." His sad smile brought an immediate softening to the handsome features, Drewry thought. "The War has caused us all much pain," he said quietly. "Perhaps it is best not to reopen old wounds."

"Thank you, Mr. Auburn. Some things *are* still too painful to talk about."

Chase searched her eyes for a moment and reached for the bread plate. "Could I interest you in some brown bread? Miss Beecher assures us that it is much more nutritious than the bleached-flour variety."

Drewry took a slice and couldn't resist a silent prayer of thanksgiving for this understanding man. She knew God expected truth from His children, but she sure hoped He would help her keep her awful secret . . .

ہ

Drewry loved her new room. The downy mattress of the big brass bed promised a comfortable night's sleep. When lit, the pair of crystalline lanterns that stood on each round, mahogany table flanking her bed flashed thousands of tiny rainbows on the walls and ceiling.

There was no window seat like the one in her room at Plumtree Orchards. Instead, French doors opened onto a wide, covered balcony, presenting a spectacular view of Magnolia Grange's northern horizon. The thick, blood-red Persian carpet that covered most of the pine-planked floor would provide protection from the cold when she stepped from bed on chilly mornings. And the maple chiffonier was more than large enough for storing the few dresses she'd brought from home.

Home . . .

Snuggling deeper beneath the satiny, down-stuffed comforter, Drewry sighed. Though she'd been gone less than a week, she missed Plumtree Orchards. Missed the scent of flowers that would be budding on the fruit trees. More than anything else, she missed being able to saunter out to the shed any time she pleased, where old Jeb would no doubt be stirring a vat of the home-brewed chemicals he'd invented to discourage the assault of insect attacks on the delicate plantings.

If she closed her eyes, Drewry could see his weathered, friendly face. She recalled how much Jeb resembled her grandfather, Abraham Sheffield. All she had to go on were the ferrotypes she'd found in a chest in the attic, but the similarities were striking, particularly when Jeb smiled.

She remembered, too, that each time she mentioned the likeness, Jeb's coffee-colored cheeks would darken in an embarrassed flush. "You hush, now, Miss Drew," he'd say, "an' let me get back to work."

It had been Drewry's father and Abe's son—George

Sheffield—who, despite the dangers of doing so, had taught Jeb to read and write. Had taught him to add and subtract, too, and how to maintain careful control of Plumtree inventory.

For his twenty-first birthday, George's father had given him five hundred acres of rocky bottomland. Abe's thought was that if his son could make things grow in that near-useless soil, he was a farmer, indeed.

At great financial expense, George had imported the saplings of fruit trees from South America, the Caribbean Islands, and from as far away as India. At great emotional expense, he'd endured the scoffing of fellow farmers who expected and predicted his complete and utter failure.

George had worked side by side with his hired hands, and within five years, Plumtree Orchards was out-producing Abe's corn and wheat farm. Within ten years, because he'd had the foresight to add new trees and vines to his product line every season, he was supplying canneries up and down the eastern seaboard with fruits of every variety. And Jeb had been right, every step of the way. "Like brothers, we was," Jeb had told Drewry once. "But y'all don't tell nobody I said dat," he cautioned, a worried frown creasing his brow.

She had wondered what worried him, what dark secret he was hiding. But Drewry understood his fear, especially now that she was hiding a dark secret of her own. She missed his homespun advice. She yearned to hear again his voice, filtering softly from his room on the third floor of the manor house, crooning sweetly as she drifted off to sleep.

"I's lucky I can sleep in the big house," he admitted to her early one morning as they sat alone in the kitchen, sipping coffee. "If I wasn't a mulatto, I'd sleep down in the cottages, like the other Nigras."

Not that the other servants were treated poorly; Abraham and George had always been good to their hired help, building sturdy houses and giving each a parcel of land on which to plant family favorites. They had also provided medical care in time of illness and paid fair wages.

After the War, when all slaves were freed, George had taught them to manage their income by allowing them to invest in Plumtree Orchards. When times were good, he gave his help their share of the profits so that they were able to build up a modest savings. Some bought land. Others started businesses of their own. Most, however, were content to stay on at Plumtree Orchards, where they were guaranteed a home . . . and respect.

Jeb had always said that he wanted to be buried near Gunpowder River. "So I can hear the water rushin' over the rocks." Drewry had made a solemn vow to see that his wish was fulfilled. But how would she keep her promise, from way down south in Richmond?

Tears welled up in her eyes. Angrily, she swiped them away. "Someday," she whispered into the darkness. "I'll come home someday, Jeb. And when I do, I'll take care of you the way you took care of me ever since Uncle James . . . ."

To finish the thought was simply too painful. Uncle James had been so protective, so loving . . . that is, until he returned from the War. Drewry had prayed, as she tended her uncle's injuries, that he'd be his kind, fun-loving self again soon. His horribly wounded left foot began to heal, and though he walked with a limp and was forced to get about by leaning on a cane, his body repaired itself.

But his heart and his soul seemed scarred beyond repair. It was as though the grisly sights and sounds he'd witnessed on the battlefield had clung to him. Unable to keep down much more than warm soup and bread, he lost weight. And he insisted that the only way he could get any sleep at all was to empty a bottle of red-eye whiskey.

Soon, he was drinking in the daytime, too. "Every time I blink, I see 'em, lying all around me," he would ramble between swallows. Before long, Drewry's dear Uncle James was unrecognizable to her. Disheveled and rumpled, he limped about the house and grounds, reeking of alcohol, cursing and complaining at every turn. He became abusive to the hired hands. Abusive, even to Jeb who, thanks to the lessons he'd learned at Abe's knee, had been responsible for keeping Plumtree Orchards financially secure.

Jeb had endured it all without a word of complaint. "Why don't you just leave here?" Drewry tearfully asked him after one of James's particularly violent outbursts. "You're free now. Why don't you just go?"

"Can't leave," he'd said in his quiet, slow way. "Who'd look out for you an' the others?"

Drewry sighed. Unable to sleep, she climbed out of the warm, soft bed and tiptoed to the narrow French doors. Outside, on the balcony, she hugged herself to fend off the chill of the night air.

Magnolia Grange was a magnificent place. But it wasn't home. Chase Auburn seemed like a kind and decent man, but he wasn't family. She'd been angry with Uncle James hundreds of times—each time he resisted her efforts to help in his recuperation—but she'd never hated him; remembering what he'd been like before kept her love for him alive.

After he'd frittered away nearly every dime Plumtree Orchards earned, he had taken to gambling to meet his ever-rising alcohol needs, then had sold off most of their lovely furnishings to pay his gambling debts. And when there was nothing worth betting on left anywhere at Plumtree, he'd handed Drewry over like property, costing her the only home she'd ever known and depriving her of her oldest and dearest friend as well.

"Oh, how I miss you, Jeb," she said aloud, biting back bitter tears. "Will I ever see you again?"

five

Drewry didn't know how long she'd been asleep when the piercing screams woke her. She grabbed her thick chenille robe and belted it around her waist as she ran down the hall toward Sally's room.

The child shrieked, pointing to her window. On the grounds below came the sound of horses whinnying, men shouting. A gunshot rang out.

Drewry was torn by indecision. Should she investigate the ruckus or embrace the terrified child? Just then, Sam ran into the room on bare feet and buried his tear-streaked face in the folds of Drewry's robe. The choice was simple—the children came first.

Drewry lifted Sam into her arms and deposited him on the bed beside his sister, then joined the little tykes in the center of the fluffy feather mattress. Drawing Sally and Sam into a warm embrace, she crooned, "There, there, it's all right."

But obviously, it wasn't. The shouts of angry voices intensified. Another gunshot pierced the night. Suddenly, things grew ominously still.

"I'm going to peek out the window to see what's going on," Drewry whispered, "but I'll be back quick as can be to tell you what I've seen." She leaned back slightly and gazed into four frightened eyes. "You'll stay right here?"

Sally grabbed Drewry's hand. "Don't go out there," the child pleaded. "Something bad could happen to you."

Drewry gave her a reassuring hug. "I won't be out of your sight, even for a minute," she promised. She ruffled the children's hair. "Aren't you the least bit curious to know what all the fuss and bother is about?"

Sam nodded. "Is Papa out there?"

"If he is," Drewry said softly, "I'll tell you." She remembered how secure it had made her feel when Uncle James had told her the truth about her puppy and the death of her parents.

Drewry scooted off the bed and hurried to the window, being careful to stay hidden behind the curtains. The scene that greeted her eyes was terrifying.

Six men on horseback, each carrying a fiery torch, surrounded Chase. Claib and Simon stood on either side of him, half-aiming their shotguns at the menacing men. Their horses, draped in white sheets, stomped blanketed hooves on the gravel drive. Skulls gleamed white in the moonlight and grinned garishly from their resting places on the saddle horns.

The men, wearing long, white robes and tall pointed white hats, taunted Chase: "Nigger-lover! Turncoat!" The round eyeholes cut into their hoods made them appear even more frightening. "How dare you teach them darkies of yours to read an' write! It's agin the law!"

"It's legal now," Chase countered, fists doubled up at his sides. "Now get off my property."

The biggest man dismounted, brandishing his torch. "Where's your loyalty, man?" he demanded. "You're a Virginian, not a Yankee. Ain't no Yankee law can change how the South feels about slaves."

"Thousands of men gave their lives in the name of freedom," Chase responded. "I'll not dishonor their sacrifice by upholding heathen rituals."

"Heathen!" the giant yelled. "Why, the White Brotherhood follows God's Word to the letter. We're tryin' to *save* the South, not harm it, you idiot!"

"I've read about your little 'society,'" Chase snapped. "You murder and rape and burn . . . all in the name of Jesus. You're thugs, that's all you are. You're a threat to all that's good and decent in the South!"

"We ain't gonna allow nobody to ruin what it's taken more'n a century to build up. Folks like *you* are the threat, Chase Auburn, with your high-falootin' ways. Teachin niggers to read an' write, tryin' to grow peas an' carrots where cotton an' tobacco always grew. What are you tryin' to do, man? Where's your respect for tradition?"

Chase stood silent for a long moment, both arms crossed over his chest. "I can't respect any tradition rooted in lies and violence. Now get off my land before I fetch my shotgun."

The big man swung into his saddle. "This here's been a friendly warnin', Auburn. You'll get back on the straight and narrow . . . and stay there . . . or you'll be sorry. You're gonna stop tryin' to make Yankees of us all. You'll pay Old Virginee respect, even if we have to beat it into you!"

Chase reached up and grabbed a corner of the man's robe and pulled. "No man who has to hide beneath a bedsheet scares me. You're a yellow-bellied coward." He looked at the rest of them, one at a time. "You're *all* cowards. Now for the last time, *get off my land!*"

The big man signaled his followers. "We'll be going, but this is not the last you'll see of us. And believe me, next time you'll be sorry!" On that note of warning, he spun his horse around and charged down the long, winding drive, his men whooping and hollering behind.

❧

Drewry, hands over her wildly thumping heart, turned from the window. In the minute or two that passed as she watched, she could no more deny her fear for Chase than cease breathing. The way he had stood his ground, unflinching . . . The strength of his voice and stance reminded her of the way Uncle James had been . . . once.

But she also feared anew for *herself.* "I can't respect any tradition rooted in lies," he had said. How long would it be before he learned the truth about her? How long?

Shaking off the horror of what she had heard, Drewry climbed into the center of Sally's wide bed and gathered the children close. At least, she would tell *them* the truth, but only as much as they needed to hear, and in language they could understand.

"Seems your father has had some . . . gentlemen callers," she began cautiously, "who don't quite agree with the kinds of seeds he plants. They were trying to convince him that he ought to plant nothing but cotton and tobacco, like everybody else in Richmond."

"But why were they shouting?" Sam asked, his voice trembling.

"Oh," Drewry replied with a nonchalant wave of her hand, "some men just like to make a lot of noise." She gave a little laugh, more for the children's sake than to express any levity she felt. "I guess they want to make sure everybody hears what they have to say."

❧

The moment the riders were out of sight, Chase ran into the house and up the stairs. When he passed Sam's room, the empty bed alarmed him . . . until he heard his son's voice coming from Sally's room. It was then that he heard Drewry's voice, soft and reassuring, ". . . I guess they want to make sure everybody hears what they have to say."

Chase leaned against the wall and crossed one booted foot over the other. Despite his recent confrontation with the hooded men, he smiled as he eavesdropped on the new nanny and her small charges.

"Are the men gonna hurt Papa?" Sally asked.

"Your father is big and strong and smarter than all those men put together," Drewry responded quickly. "They're going to have to do a lot more than holler and yell to hurt *him!*"

She hadn't lied to his daughter, Chase noticed, yet she'd made Sally believe that he was safe from the night visitors' threats.

"They said they'd be back," Sally stated, remembering. "Will they come in the dark again? Will they come *soon?*"

Chase heard Drewry's long, deep sigh. "Sally, my sweet, I'm sure they won't want to climb out of their nice warm beds!"

"Where's Papa?" Sam wanted to know.

"I'm right here." Chase strode into the room and stood beside the bed. "Do you children realize it's past midnight?" He gave Drewry a wink as he gathered the boy into his arms.

But Sam was still obviously distressed. "Will the bad men come back tonight, Papa?"

"No, son. They won't be back. Now, what do you say we get you tucked into bed?"

"I'll do it." Drewry rose from Sally's bed and held out her arms, waiting for Chase to hand over his son.

He shook his head. "Thank you, but I'd rather do it myself, if you don't mind." Chase walked nearer the bed and leaned over to kiss Sally's cheek. "Good night, sweet child," he whispered. "May the Good Lord grant you beautiful dreams and send a legion of angels to watch over you."

"G'night, Papa." Sally smiled sleepily and wrapped her arms around her father's neck.

Straightening, Chase headed for the door, pausing to say, "I'd like a word with you in my library, Drewry."

Drewry's heart pounded. *What could he possibly want at this hour?* "Yes sir. I'll be down just as soon as I've tucked Sally in."

Much as she tried, Drewry scarcely heard a word the child said once Chase left the room. Did he know about her deception? Had the agency contacted him to check on the new nanny they had sent him? Would he demand an explanation for her deceit? Would he insist upon her immediate resignation?

As if through a fog, Drewry listened to the little girl's prayers—for the second time that night—gave her a hug and a kiss, and promised to take them both for a long walk in the morning. But she knew that no matter which direction they went on their excursion, it wouldn't be nearly as long and difficult a trip as her descent down the winding staircase that led to Chase's library.

&

Drewry made a quick stop in her own room to slip into a simple cotton dress. "Ain't fittin' nor proper for a young lady to be flittin' about in her nightclothes," Jeb's wife Missy would have said.

"I couldn't help overhearing what you said to the children," Chase began, motioning to her to take the tufted brown leather chair opposite his as soon as she entered the room. "I must say, I was quite impressed with your aplomb tonight."

Drewry breathed a sigh of relief. Perhaps she hadn't been found out, after all . . .

Chase stood and began pacing the length of the library, his boots thudding softly on the thick Oriental carpet.

"Who were those men?" she asked, wide-eyed.

"They call themselves the White Brotherhood. The Society of the White Rose. The Ku Klux Klan. There are many interesting names for their little . . . *club*." Chase spat out the last word as if it were a mouthful of spoiled meat. "But they're nothing more than a gang of bullies."

"If their goal is to terrorize, they've succeeded." Drewry sighed. "Skulls and crossbones . . . torches . . . muskets . . ." She shuddered at the memory of the white-sheeted hoodlums. "And those awful, awful masks . . ."

Chase laughed softly and returned to his seat. "Yes, they're a sorry sight, all right."

"'Ku Klux Klan,'" Drewry repeated. "What sort of language is that?"

"It's Greek, and it means 'circle.' They hope to impress upon us how well-organized they are—impenetrable from the outside, inescapable from the inside. Their symbol is a cross within the circle, to prove they're doing God's work, which is the greatest irony of all. In persecuting Christ's people, they are persecuting the Lord Himself."

Drewry remembered Christ's words to Paul on a similar mission along the Damascus road: "Saul, Saul, why do you persecute me?"

Chase settled back in the chair. "When they first started raiding the countryside, their aim was to have us believe they were the discontented spirits of dead Confederate soldiers, out to seek vengeance upon those for whom they died in vain. That's why they hide behind white gowns and hoods."

Drewry leaned forward with a frown on her face. "I heard one of the men say they were doing God's work. Why, the very idea! I'd like to see them point out the verse in the Bible that gives them permission to commit murder and mayhem!" She took a deep breath and continued her tirade. "I've read newspaper articles about their kind, and they think nothing of lynching innocent people, burning them out of house and home . . . and worse!"

"Enough talk of dark deeds," said Chase. Standing, he held out his hand to her. "Why don't we go into the kitchen and see if there's any milk left from supper. Perhaps you'll warm us both a cup to settle our nerves."

For a minute there, in Sally's room, Drewry feared he'd uncovered her bluff. Now, almost weak with relief, she put her hand into his as he helped her to her feet.

"My old nanny used to float a pat of butter on our warm milk," she said, walking beside him through the quiet house.

"Is that so?"

Realizing that she had betrayed herself, Drewry withdrew her hand hastily. *You little ninny!* she scolded herself. *You've gone and admitted you were once well off enough to afford a nanny of your own!* "My guardian," she explained carefully, "owned a sizable farm before the War."

"Ah, yes," Chase said, lighting the lamp that hung above the kitchen table. "That abominable War. It cost your guardian a great deal, then?"

Drewry opened the back door, stepped out onto the porch, and reached into the wood-lined iron box where she'd seen Matilda store the pitcher of milk. "Yes," she said truthfully, shutting the door. "He barely escaped with his life."

Chase placed two heavy white mugs on the table, then sat on one of the stools stored beneath it as Drewry poured milk into the copper kettle on the stove. "You said you were quite young when you lost your parents. Did they leave you in the care of this guardian?"

Drewry nodded, then struck a match and fired up the stove. "Yes. He's my father's brother." In her mind's eye, she saw Uncle James again—tall, dark-bearded, handsome, full of life. In that instant, however, she pictured him as she'd seen him last—rumpled and red-eyed, flailing his cane like a sword . . .

"You handled things quite admirably tonight," Chase said quietly. "I'm sure the children were very upset when they heard all the ruckus outside."

"Yes," she admitted, "they were terrified, at first. But I think they'll be fine as long as we're honest with them."

Chase nodded his agreement. "I've always felt it's far easier to deal with fact than fantasy. My dear departed mother—we lost her to pleurisy last year—practically insisted we tell Sally that her mother was not dead, only asleep." He scowled, then added, "When Sam grew old enough to understand, were we to tell him the same lie? And what were the children to think when their mother never woke up? How was I to explain _that_?"

Drewry tilted the kettle left and right to help the milk heat evenly, hearing the hiss. She searched the cupboards for a bit of butter before finding it in a crock on the fancifully carved wood shelf.

"My uncle was quite straightforward with me when my parents were killed. Knowing how they died was easier to bear that wondering what had happened to them. I'm sure my acceptance of being orphaned was a direct result of his honesty."

"And just how *did* they die, Drewry?"

She met his gaze, warm and brown and understanding. Grasping the kettle's blue-flowered ceramic handle with a crocheted potholder, Drewry stepped up to the table and filled their mugs. The milk bubbled and steamed, and as the dollop of butter she added began to melt, tiny golden circles floated atop the foamy white surface. She used the butter spoon to stir her milk, then handed a mug to Chase and sat down across from him.

She'd have to tread carefully here—give him enough information to satisfy his curiosity, yet not so much that he'd be able to track down her family. "Mama and Papa had gone to Baltimore on business," she began cautiously, keeping her eyes downcast. "A snake in the road frightened the horses, and their carriage . . . overturned and . . ."

Chase halted her before she could continue. "I'm sorry, Drewry. I shouldn't have asked." He sipped his milk, studying her solicitously. "So tell me, what do you think of your new home?"

She met his eyes then. "Oh, your house is simply lovely."

He returned her warm smile. Then, wrapping his hands around his mug, he added, "And your room . . . is it to your liking? We could move the furnishings or . . ."

"Oh, no! I wouldn't change a thing. I'm sure I'll be quite happy here," she assured him. "I'm only hoping that I'll be able to help you make those beautiful children of yours feel content and protected, always."

It seemed to be just what he needed to hear, for the sparkle returned to his dark eyes. He downed the last of his milk, then rose. "It's very late. Perhaps we'd best get some sleep now."

At the door, he paused and glanced over his shoulder. "Good night, Drewry," he said softly. "And thank you. . . ."

She opened her mouth to question why he was thanking her, but he was gone. Suddenly, the kitchen, which had seemed bright and cozy before, now felt chilly. The answer would have to wait until morning. Meanwhile, she'd have to make it through the remainder of this long, strange night . . . alone.

ъ

Magnolia Grange
Richmond, Virginia
March, 1968

Dear Jeb,

I'm sorry it's taken me so long to write you, but things have been so busy here.

You'll be happy to hear that I have found myself a home—at least for now. I met a girl on the southbound train who was traveling to Virginia to become the nanny for a rich man's children. Well, as it turned out, the "nanny" met up with a soldier, and they're married by now, I suppose. So your Drewry has assumed her position—unbeknownst to my new employer, unfortunately.

I am in a place near Richmond, Virginia, known as Magnolia Grange, a magnificent plantation owned by a Mr. Chase Auburn. He is working on some crop experiments. If Mr. Auburn (he insists I call him Chase) succeeds in getting his soy beans and hothouse plants on the market, he'll be a very rich man indeed, for he'll be able to sell his produce locally and save on the cost of having the goods shipped in.

I have more or less settled into my new home.

My, but how grand Magnolia Grange is! You would love the gardens here, Jeb. There are daffodils and tulips of every color of the rainbow in bloom already—imported, I'm told, from Holland. The children say I've missed the crocus season, but they say more will bloom in the fall. I expect I'll be here to see those . . . if my small deception is not discovered first.

If only it were possible for you to meet my delightful charges! Sally is six, and has her father's dark eyes and hair. Matilda (who's the <u>real</u> boss around here), tells me that Sam will be four come November. Sam, says Matilda, looks like his mama—golden brown hair and hazel eyes and an angel's smile. They're such sweet children, Jeb. Taking care of them is my job, I suppose, but it no chore at all. I believe I'm going to enjoy it here very much.

It seems so long since I last saw you. I yearn to hear you sing a sad old ballad. And I sure could use some of your down-to-earth advice. I hope Uncle James isn't making life too unbearable for you and Missy these days. You'll write me soon, won't you, and let me know how you're getting on? Tell me, too, how old Porter took the news that his bride-to-be had escaped on the morning train!

Until I hear from you, please know that you're in my thoughts and prayers always.

With my fondest affection,
Drewry

"What's Sheriff Kelly doin' here?" Matilda asked, peeking through the lacy white curtain in the front parlor. "He's the wustest-mannered man east of the Miss'ippi." She stood back and planted chubby fists on her wide-spread hips.

"Why, he left his horse right out in the middle of the yard! Now who's gonna clean up after the beast?"

She grimaced when he pounded on the front door. "Dear Lawd," Matilda muttered, waddling into the foyer, "give me the strength to keep a civil tongue in my head whilst he be a guest in Mistah Auburn's home."

Drewry looked on in fascination as Matilda ranted. She listened, more fascinated still as the housekeeper greeted him: "Why, Sheriff Kelly, what you be doin' in these here parts? Seem like ages since I see you las'."

Alden Kelly bristled under Matilda's syrupy scrutiny. "Where's Chase?" he demanded. "I need to speak to him, right now."

"Well, suh, do come in," Matilda sang, "an' set yo'sef down in the parlor an' take a load off those feets o' yours whilst I fetch 'im." Behind his back, she rolled her eyes and made a face at Drewry. But her countenance was benign once again when Alden Kelly turned to seat himself on the plush green divan. "Kin I git ya somethin', Sheriff? Maybe a cup o' tea?"

"Just get Chase in here," he snorted.

Drewry inhaled sharply, recognizing Kelly's gravelly voice as the one belonging to the leader of the White Brotherhood. She shivered involuntarily and stepped past him toward the foyer.

"Hold up just a minute, there, Matilda," Kelly said. "Who's this pretty young thing?"

Matilda stepped in front of Drewry protectively. "Why, this be Miss Sheffield, Sheriff—Mistuh Chase's new nanny. She gonna take care of Sally an' Sam. Gonna teach 'em to read an' write an' cipher numbers. Ain't that right, Miss Drew?"

Drewry, thankful for the security of the woman's nearness, nodded.

Kelly squinted appraisingly. "Got a feller?"

"'Course she ain't," Matilda answered for her. "She ain't gonna git no feller no time soon, neither, 'cause Mistah Chase, he be wantin' her to get busy educatin' his younguns. Ain't that right, Miss Drew?"

Again Drewry nodded dumbly.

"Why don't you go on upstairs an' find Mistah Chase, Miss Drew, whilst I puts on a kettle o' water, jus' in case he be wantin' a cup o' tea whilst he an' the sheriff here talk."

Gratefully, Drewry escaped up the steps. She found Chase in his library, poring over another of his thick agriculture text-books. Surprised by her sudden appearance, he looked up and smiled. "Well, what brings you here?" He leaned back in his leather chair. "Haven't seen you since—" he glanced at his pocket watch—"since breakfast, at least half an hour ago."

Without asking permission, Drewry slid the library's pocket doors shut. "Matilda said I should let you know you have a visitor." She wrung her hands in front of her.

"Oh?" Chase stood to his feet.

"It's Sheriff Kelly. I recognized his voice . . . He's . . ."

Chase walked around to the front of his desk and patted her shoulder. "Now, now. Calm yourself, Drewry."

"But he was here last night. The leader of that gang . . ."

"There's nothing to worry about. Trust me."

She sighed deeply. "But he's such a vile and vicious man. What if . . ."

Chase turned and walked toward the door. "Why don't we find out what brought him all the way out to Magnolia Grange this time?"

Drewry's feet seemed frozen to the spot. But when Chase opened the doors and entered the foyer, Drewry found the strength to move; she couldn't leave him alone with that horrible man. What if the sheriff tried to harm her new employer? What if he threatened him again? *Well*, Drewry decided, *this time Chase will have a witness!*

"Alden Kelly," Chase said as he strode into the parlor, "what can I do for you this fine morning?"

"I've been gettin' complaints about you, Auburn," Kelly spat, leaning forward in the big armchair near the fireplace. "Folks don't like the way your niggers traipse around town like they own the place."

Chase frowned. "I'll thank you not to use that word in my home, Sheriff."

"What word?" Kelly sneered. "Oh, you mean *nigger*?"

Chase leveled him a stern look but did not reply. "Now why don't you tell me why you're here."

"Told you already. No true Virginian likes an uppity nigger."

Drewry stepped timidly into the room and sat as near Chase as the seating arrangement allowed. She squared her shoulders and lifted her chin, then cast a defiant glare in Kelly's direction.

There was a dangerous glint in Chase's eyes, despite his cool grin as he replied, "I wasn't aware that being uppity was against the law."

Kelly shot to his feet. "You've been warned, Auburn. But only 'cause my wife insisted on it. She's a God-fearin' woman who believes every man deserves a fair shake. If not for her, I wouldn't have bothered to come here today at all."

Chase stood, too. "Be sure to thank your good wife for me."

Almost casually, he glanced at Drewry, who was still sitting stiff and solemn in the chair beside the sofa. "I don't believe you've met the newest member of our family . . ."

Kelly waved an impatient hand in the air. "Yeah, yeah. Yer nigger woman intro—"

"You'll kindly refrain from referring to Matilda in that way," Chase interrupted. "She's the manager of my household and as such, deserves your respect."

"No nigger deserves re—"

The ominous look in Chase's eye silenced the sheriff. "Then I'm afraid I'll have to ask you to leave."

At this, Drewry rose, just in time to see Alden Kelly line up with Chase. Toe to toe, the men glared at each other.

Kelly was shorter than Chase by at least two inches, but carried at least fifty extra pounds around his middle. *Put there by drink and gluttony, no doubt*, Drewry surmised, frowning in disgust.

"You'd better quit actin' like a Yankee," Kelly said, wagging his stubby forefinger under Chase's nose, "or you're gonna be sorry."

"And if you don't stop abusing your powers, *you'll* be sorry."

"Me?" Kelly's wicked laughter ricocheted off the walls. "Why should *I* be sorry?"

Chase's eyes narrowed dangerously, as did his voice. "Because *some* folks around here *don't* agree with your strong-armed tactics, and if they found out what kind of clothing you wear when you call on your neighbors at night, they'd be mighty distressed. You might even have a hard time summoning votes in the next election, even if you *paid* for them, as I'm told you did in the last one . . ."

Kelly coughed and sputtered, then said through clenched teeth, "You're out of your mind, man. Who d'ya think folks is gonna believe—the feller who puts his life on the line every day to keep law and order in their town, or some high-falootin' rich man, plantin' Yankee crops. It's your word against mine, and I'll . . ."

"Sheriff Kelly," Drewry said in a honeyed tone, "I wonder if you could tell me about the emblem on your . . . costume. What does it mean?"

"Uh . . . emblem? Costume? What costume?"

"Why, the one sewn on your white robe, of course."

Kelly scowled. "Women," he puffed, shaking his head, "should be seen and not heard."

Drewry arched her brow. "I've never heard the term 'high-falootin' before . . . but I heard it last night. And just a moment ago, you said it again. I've never heard a cough quite like yours, either. You really ought to see a doctor."

"What is she babblin' about?" Kelly demanded, turning to Chase.

"I believe she's saying that she could testify in a court of law that she recognizes you as part of the gang that was here last night," he replied evenly.

"I . . . uh . . . I don't know what you're talkin' about, either of you," the sheriff sputtered. "I think you're both a bubble off plumb, that's what I think!" He jammed his hat back on his head and headed for the door. "Just remember, you've been warned, Auburn," he said, then slammed the door behind him.

Chase and Drewry stood side by side in the parlor, listening as Kelly's horse clattered down the gravel drive. When the sounds of his exit were no longer audible, Chase faced her. "That was a very brave thing you did just now. It means a great deal to know that you're so devoted to Magnolia Grange . . ."

Drewry blushed, inordinately pleased with his compliment.

"But I'm afraid it wasn't very smart." His frown disturbed the perfect symmetry of his strong brow. "Alden Kelly isn't someone you want for an enemy."

Stunned by this sudden change of attitude, Drewry faked a brave smile. "Why, I can't think of a single person I *would* want as an enemy!"

"This is no laughing matter," Chase went on, his tone severe. "The man is insane, along with the crowd that follows him. There's no telling what they might do to spread their message of hatred. No telling what violence they'd be willing to resort to . . ."

He sighed deeply. "You've put yourself in grave danger, interfering like that, and in so doing, you've also put my children at risk."

Drewry blinked rapidly. "I—I'm so sorry. I didn't realize . . . I never thought . . ."

To her surprise, he reached for her and drew her into a protective hug. Her heart hammered as she rested her head on his chest and listened to his soothing words. "I'm sorry if I've frightened you, Drewry. But I had to make you understand that you must weigh every decision you make carefully; everything you do from here on out will, in one way or another, affect my children.

"I know what you were trying to do, and I thank you from the bottom of my heart for your loyalty. But I can take care of myself. Your first responsibility is the children." Chase released his hold and stepped away. "Incidentially, where *are* the children?"

"They—they're . . . out back . . . I think," she finished in a whispery voice.

He took a deep breath. "Go to them, then, while I give some thought to how we're going to handle Kelly and his rowdy boys."

Drewry so wanted to take good care of Sally and Sam, and already she'd failed. "I—I'm so sorry," she said again, biting back tears.

"Don't be sorry," he said, heading back toward the sanctuary of his library. "Be *careful*."

He was right. She couldn't deny that. What she'd intended as a good deed had been anything but that. Drewry was left—

once again—with the inescapable fact that she'd proven herself unworthy.

And if unworthy . . . then no wonder she was so unlovable!

&

Claib hummed quietly as he flicked the whip over the strong backs of the pair of matched horses drawing Chase's grand carriage. The blacks picked up their pace.

"What you be buyin' in town today, Miss Drew?" Matilda inquired curiously.

"Fabric, I hope. I plan to make Sally a dress for her birthday party."

Matilda nodded. "Only yestiddy, she tole me she ain't got a proper party dress." She gave Drewry a sidelong look. "Her fav'rite color be blue, you know, same as her mama's."

"Thank you, Matilda. I don't know what I'd do without you to help me care for Sam and Sally."

Matilda drew herself up proudly, her eyes on Claib's back. "L'il Sam, his fav'rite color be red. Like Mistuh Chase."

Drewry giggled. "Why, I would have figured Chase for a 'gray' man or even black. Something dignified and gentlemanly . . ."

Matilda slapped her thighs and leaned back, her hearty laughter interrupting Drewry's comment.

"'Tilda," Claib called over his shoulder, "you hesh up back there, 'fore you scare the horses, y'heah?"

Matilda made a feeble attempt to compose herself, as she wiped the tears from her eyes. "Miss Drew, if you think Mistah Chase be a dignified gent, you don't know him like I do."

Drewry smiled into the broad black face, thinking, *Oh, but I wish I did!*

"Mistah Chase weren't no easy youngun to raise," Matilda continued confidentially. "Why, that boy, he could find mischief just about anyplace. Ain't that right, Claib?" she asked, poking her old friend's shoulder.

"Yep," Claib agreed, snickering. "Mistah Chase, he be one onery l'il tike, all right."

Drewry shook her head. "But he's so proper and distinguished. I'd never have believed he could be anything else, even as a boy!"

This time, Claib's laughter joined Matilda's. When the sound died away, the black woman was entirely serious. "Miss Drew, the man you sees today am the man Miss T'resa made of him."

Drewry frowned. "His wife? Didn't she like him the way he was?" Drewry found that hard to believe since, in her mind, Chase was the most nearly perfect man she'd ever met.

Matilda shook her head. "She like him just fine. But Miss T'resa, she be a God-lovin' woman, an' she tame Mistah Chase right down, she did."

"Made a silk purse outta a sow's ear," Claib agreed.

"Them two be mighty happy," Matilda added thoughtfully. "Why, I never seen a man smile like he done when she say they gonna have a baby." Matilda clasped her hands in front of her ample bosom. "An' he cry like a baby when she lef' this world. Why, I believe he cried a bucket o' tears. Ain't that right, Claib?"

He nodded solemnly.

"He walk 'round de house like a man who died hisself," Matilda continued. "Hardly touch his food. Barely say a word to nobody, 'cept them younguns." She sighed heavily. "Then he went back to church, 'cause Paster Tillman tole him he best take control of himself before the chil'rens had no mama . . . *and* no papa.

"So Mistah Chase, he take to prayin' mos' all day. It seem to help keep him calm through the daylight hours. But at night . . ." Matilda drew an embroidered handkerchief from her handbag and dabbed at her teary eyes. "I don't believe I ever heard such mournful wailin' as what come from his bedchamber. Broke my heart to hear him weep like that."

Claib nodded. "Plumb pitiful, all right."

"I know something 'bout losin' loved ones," Matilda interrupted. "Lost my man while our only youngun was still inside me. Lost that youngun during the War. He be a Buffalo soldier . . ."

While Matilda's sad story moved Drewry's heart, her thoughts turned to Chase. It was hard to imagine that just three years ago, this strong and capable man had nearly given in to his grief. Drewry felt a deep and abiding compassion for him, and though he was her employer and their relationship was not likely to progress beyond that, a glimmer of hope that it *could* be more—much more —swelled within her. They had more in common than the care and well-being of his children. They had both loved and lost people who were central to their lives.

"I hope someone will love me that way someday," she blurted out. Then, as if regretting her impulsive words, Drewry readjusted the folds of her skirt and added, "Though I'm aware I'm destined to become an old maid."

"Shucks, Miss Drew," Claib said, "seem to me you jus' the marryin' age. 'Sides, you ain't all silly an' giggly, you know the value of a dollar, an' you have a heart the size of all Virginee."

Matilda nodded in agreement. "Not only that, chile, but you's honest as the day is long!"

Drewry felt her cheeks grow pale. Nothing about her life these days was honest. She knew that the Scriptures talked about building a house on a firm foundation if it were to endure. But she'd built her life in Virginia on a foundation of lies. It was only a matter of time before her entire world came tumbling down.

Unaware of her distress, Matilda talked on. "An' if you want my 'pinion, you's a sight prettier than most. Why, any man worth his salt can see that right off."

You've no right burdening these good people with your dreams and wishes, Drewry reprimanded herself. *And if you had one ounce of honesty in you, you'd tell them the whole truth!* For an instant, Drewry considered doing just that. "Confession is good for the soul," Jeb used to say . . .

But Matilda interrupted her soul-searching. "I'll let you in on a little secret, if you promise to keep it to yo'sef," she whispered, mischief glinting in her dark eyes.

Curious, Drewry put aside her urge to confess and leaned near.

"Well, I recollect the way Mistah Chase used to look at Miss T'resa 'fore they married. His eyes would shine an' he'd stare— till somebody caught him at it." Matilda chuckled softly. "Got all tongue-tied 'round her, too."

Drewry swallowed the stinging sensation of envy that bubbled inside her at the thought of Chase looking longingly at his beloved. She felt uncomfortable with those feelings, couldn't imagine why she'd be feeling this way; he was her employer, after all, and nothing more. Besides, didn't the man have a perfect right to moon over the woman he loved?

But Matilda, oblivious to Drewry's dark musings, grinned at her as she whispered, "Mistah Chase like you, Miss Drew. I kin tell."

The only thing Drewry could remember was the gentle scolding he had given her that morning, after Sheriff Kelly's hasty departure. "Well, I—I hope so. I like him, too. He's a very kind man . . . and a—a fine father . . ."

Matilda elbowed Drewry in the ribs. "That's not what I's talkin' 'bout, Miss Drew. I means . . . Mistuh Chase like you . . . the way a man like a *woman*."

"True enough," Claib agreed, eavesdropping from his seat up front. "Plenty o' times, I seen him lookin' at you . . . dat way."

Drewry gasped. Were they both daft? she wondered. How could this be? But a quiet note of joy sang in her heart at the possibility that Chase might think of her as more than a mere employee. "I—I don't know what to say."

"No need to say nothin', Miss Drew," Matilda said, the wisdom of her years echoing in her tone. "Jus' keep bein' yo'self." Again she poked the driver in the back. "Ain't that right, Claib?"

The conversation was quickly forgotten as Claib slowed the carriage on Richmond's bustling Cary Street. Everywhere they looked, construction was under way. These new buildings, Drewry knew, were to replace the once-sturdy structures that had been destroyed during the War. She tried to visualize this lovely cobbled street as it had been before cannonball blasts had uprooted nearby trees and gouged out craters. But all Drewry was able to see was the image of Uncle James, and the devastation he had suffered—every bit as uprooted and damaged as the landscape.

"You ready to go inside, Miss Drew?" Matilda asked as she climbed down from the carriage, abruptly ending Drewry's reverie.

"Oh! Of course!" Drewry hurried to join her on the plank sidewalk just as Claib came around to help.

He scratched his head in confusion. "Miss Drew, I's sposed to hep you down from up there."

With a snort and a grunt, Matilda shushed him. "We done jus' fine by oursefs. Now git on over to the feed an' grain an' see if them seeds Mistah Chase ordered done come in."

Claib nodded and headed across the street. "I'll be back here to collect y'all in an hour. Don't keep me waitin' now, Tilda, y'heah?"

"I do declare," Matilda said, clucking her tongue, "dat man is 'bout as onery as they come." She tugged at the store's screen door, then stepped aside to let Drewry enter first.

Drewry rooted through the fabric bin and finally selected several yards of pale blue organza for Sally's party dress. White lace trim, she decided, and a black velvet bow at the collar would dress the frock up nicely.

It was as she lay her purchases on the counter that Drewry noticed the tall bookshelves that lined the back wall. *I don't believe my good fortune!* she said to herself as she headed for the books—a variety of leather-bound volumes.

Drewry recalled the first novels she'd ever read, *Angelina Luxmore* and *The Life of a Beauty.* When she outgrew her taste for what she later termed "trivial works," she had turned her attention to such books as *The Vicar of Wakefield.* But Drewry had always enjoyed most the stories that captured her heart—those with a strong romantic plot.

Still, she hadn't expected to find books for sale in a general store, of all places, and surely not such a fine selection! Almost immediately, Drewry spotted a copy of Charlotte M. Yonge's *Amy Herbert.* And there, beside it, *David Copperfield.* She could almost see herself, sitting between Sam and Sally on the veranda at Magnolia Grange, inhaling multiflora roses and sipping mint tea as she read to the children from what had been her favorites.

Almost as an afterthought, she grabbed a copy of *Tristam Shandy.* She'd read that one alone in her room at night just before she drifted off to sleep. And just for good measure, she added *Ministering Children* to the growing stack of books in her arms, remembering how great an effect it had had on her as a child.

"Did you leave somethin' for somebody else, Miss Drew?" Matilda teased as Drewry plopped her treasures onto the counter.

"Thank you ever so much for inviting me to accompany you to town!" she exclaimed, impulsively throwing her arms around the housekeeper, the excitement in her voice sparkling in her eyes.

Matilda quickly peeled Drewry from her. As if out of habit,

the dark-skinned woman cast her eyes downward. "Ain't fittin'
to put on such a display in public, Miss Drew."

But Drewry knew better. Under the disapproving glare of
two women standing near the counter, she realized that what
wasn't "fitting" was the open display of friendship between a
black and a white. "Tish tosh," she said in her best Suzie
imitation. "I'll hug whomever I please, wherever I please,
whenever I please." With that, she wrapped Matilda in an
even tighter embrace and leaned her head on the plump shoulder.

Two sharp gasps echoed in the small storefront, and once
the women were gone, Drewry and Matilda looked at each
other. "Good riddance," Drewry muttered just before she and
the plump housekeeper burst into gales of laughter.

"Miss Drew," Matilda said, her hand on her heaving bosom,
"you an' Mistah Chase be perfect for one 'nother, 'cause you
both 'zactly alike—born troublemakers!"

For the first time since she'd left Plumtree Orchards, Drewry
felt wanted. Loved. Part of a family. Suddenly, she couldn't
wait to get back to Magnolia Grange and tell Chase about the
books she'd found. She wanted to tell him how she'd stood up
to the old biddies, too.

So she and Chase were exactly alike. It was one of the nicest
compliments anyone had ever paid her.

seven

Summer came quickly and quietly to Magnolia Grange. Before Drewry knew it, the dazzling clouds of pink and white dogwood petals had yielded to the green-gold leaves of summer. The magnolias bloomed, their heavy scent enhanced by the drifting perfume of lilacs and roses, all faithfully tended by Claib.

Drewry often taught the children their lessons out of doors, using a blanket and cushion thrown on the lawn for a schoolroom. "They seem so much more attentive when they're out in the sunshine," she told Chase during one of their evening meetings, sitting in the big leather chairs flanking the fireplace in his library. "Sam can write his full name on his slate now, plus all of the numbers up to ten."

"Is that so?" Chase's dark eyes surveyed Drewry approvingly. "I must say, my dear Miss Sheffield, you make a fine governess."

Drewry was relieved that the dim light from the oil lamp did not reveal the blush that rose to her cheeks.

"Tell me more about what you're teaching my children."

"Well, Sam's favorite piece from McGuffey's *Reader* is the rhyme of Mary and how her lamb followed her to school." She stifled a little laugh. "Now Sam wants to know if he can bring a lamb into our classroom."

Chase's rich laughter rang out, and Drewry felt a catch in her throat. *Oh, how I love that sound!* she thought. Quickly, however, lest he realize that her feelings for him ran deeper than would be seemly, she continued, "And Sally's favorite is the history of General George Washington by Mr. Weems, especially the incident concerning the cherry tree, when young George told the truth."

"Ah, that explains why Sally greeted me at the door the other day with the words, 'Father, I cannot tell a lie.'"

"Yes. I must say, that story has made quite an impression on the child."

The pair lapsed into a companionable silence. They sipped black tea and watched the flickering flames of the lanterns on the walls. Drewry did her best to keep her face and hands relaxed to hide the turmoil that raged within her.

Even a young child like Sally knows to tell the truth, yet I continue to live a lie! But how can I confess my deceit now? Chase would turn me out, I'm sure of it. An honorable man like that would not want a liar teaching his children.

Drewry blinked back the tears that threatened. The thought of being separated from her young charges tore at her heart with a force that jolted her. During the past ten weeks as their nanny, teacher, and substitute mother, she'd come to love Sally and Sam as if they were her own. She couldn't bear the thought of losing them. And what about their father?

By the warm, golden glow of the lantern, she stole a glance at Chase. He cut a dashing figure in his high leather boots, black pants, and white shirtwaist with his dark hair parted in the middle and swept back over his ears. She thought his heavy mustache made him appear older than his thirty years. Her heart stirred with tenderness.

During these magical moments in the library each evening, Drewry had delighted in their growing camaraderie. Chase often regaled her with stories of his misadventures in attempting to grow delicate hothouse plants. She laughed until tears came to her eyes. Sometimes, too, he shared his experiences as a Confederate officer, experiences which—and Drewry thanked God for this—had not left him a broken man, like Uncle James.

And always, Chase asked about his children.

Since coming to Magnolia Grange, Drewry had slipped into an easy companionship with Chase, as comfortably as she slipped her hands into a pair of well-worn gloves. In fact, she now felt she had always known him and—yes, she could admit her feelings in the privacy of her own heart—had always loved him.

And therein lay the insurmountable problem. She might have hoped he'd grow to love her, too. But how could he? He didn't really know her! Drewry tightened her grip around her mug of tea and tried to draw a little comfort from its warmth. The burden of deception grew heavier with each passing day. If he were ever to discover what she had done . . .

Despite the warmth of the summer evening, Drewry shuddered to recall the anger that had darkened Chase's face when Sheriff Kelly and his band of white-sheeted marauders had confronted him that fateful night. "Cowards!" he'd called them. "Children of the devil, the father of lies!"

The memory of Chase's searing words branded her heart. *I'm no better than they are!* she anguished. *I'm a coward and a liar to continue this charade. But what else am I to do?*

She watched Chase stare into the lantern's flame. He rubbed his hand over his strong jaw, shadowed by the day's beard, then pushed back a shock of thick, black hair. She was struck anew with his dark good looks—the sensual mouth; the straight, well-formed nose; the strong chin . . . But it was those ebony eyes that melted Drewry's heart. Whenever his gaze settled upon her, those eyes seemed to caress her very soul.

She closed her own eyes, feeling utterly miserable and ashamed at having taken advantage of this honorable man's trust. Then she lifted her chin almost imperceptibly and made a silent resolution: *I can't and I won't tell you the truth, Chase Auburn, because I can't bear to lose you.*

≈

"How many times do I have to tell you, Bridget, that it's no sin to read the Scriptures?"

Chase picked up the large, leather-bound Bible and opened it for the household's morning devotions. Across the wooden kitchen table, Bridget began to weep. Quickly, Drewry passed her a lace-edged hanky while Matilda, Simon, Claib, and the two children looked on sympathetically.

"Oh, Mister Chase, sir," Bridget said, her thin voice wavering, "back in the old country, my grandma taught me that readin' the Holy Scriptures is a sin and a crime. That kind of learnin' is only for the clergy. Sir, I don't want to go to hell." She sniffled loudly into Drewry's hanky.

"Come, come, Bridget," Chase went on. "Why would God have given us His Word if He hadn't wanted us to read it? I think your dear grandma was just a little bit mistaken."

At his remark, Bridget burst into a torrent of fresh tears.

Drewry scooted along the wooden bench, put her arm around the girl's heaving shoulders, and smoothed back the wild red locks. "Mr. Chase is right, Bridget," she said, her voice as soothing as if she were comforting one of the children after a nightmare. "Reading the Scriptures is pleasing to God."

Bridget stopped crying and regarded Drewry with red-rimmed blue eyes. "How'da ya know that, ma'am?"

"The Lord Jesus Himself told us that 'man shall not live by bread alone, but by every word that proceedeth out of the mouth of God,'" said Drewry. "You see, going to church on Sunday and hearing about Jesus is one way of growing closer to the Lord. But reading His Word for ourselves is another."

"Then . . . 'tis really not a sin?"

"Not at all," broke in Chase, his face creased in a kind and understanding smile. "It's a virtue."

For a long moment, everyone waited as Bridget considered this new idea. She took a deep breath, relieved, it seemed. "All right, then. If that's what the Lord says." She sniffled one last time, dried her eyes, and stuffed the handkerchief into the pocket of her apron. "Thank you, Miss Drewry. I'll launder your hanky before I return it." She blinked and smiled. "You're a good friend t'me, m'lady."

"And you're a good friend, too." Drewry squeezed Bridget's freckled hand.

"All right, then," said Chase. "Let's begin our devotions, shall we? Would you do us the honor of reading today's psalm, Drewry?"

Chase watched Drewry across the massive table as she read. Bridget was right. Drewry looked like a proper lady with her starched, high-necked shirtwaist and her plaid skirt. In the privacy of his own mind, Chase thought of her as his Lady Nanny.

"'Behold, thou desirest truth in the inward parts,'" Drewry read, pronouncing each word with care, "'and in the hidden part thou shalt make me to know wisdom . . .'"

Even her soft, feminine voice was ladylike, Chase thought. Obviously, Drewry had been trained in the art of elocution. More and more, Chase found himself pondering her upbringing. She had revealed so little about her past. Did she have a secret to hide? If so, what was it? What could be so terrible that she could not trust their growing friendship enough to share it with him? "Truth in the inward parts." Yes, he desired greatly to know the truth about Drewry Sheffield.

Chase shifted uncomfortably on the wooden bench, drawing a disapproving glance from Matilda, who, since he was a boy, had insisted on respectful silence during devotions. Chase grinned to himself. But he could not force his mind to focus on the words Drewry was reading. *Why?* Why could she not share her secret with him? The question had been nagging at Chase day and night, though he couldn't imagine why it mattered, one way or the other. She had proven herself more than competent as a nanny and teacher. She performed flawlessly the duties for which he paid her. Shouldn't that be sufficient? So why, then, did this irresistible urge to know about her private life haunt him?

Chase shifted his weight again. Matilda was sure to reprove him later. He reached into the pocket of his jacket to still his hands, at least. When his fingers brushed the ferrotype of Theresa, a sense of shame immediately flooded over him. How could he dishonor the memory of his beloved wife, mother of his children, by entertaining thoughts of another woman?

Bitter accusations echoed in his head like broken shutters flapping in a storm. He couldn't quiet them. At length, he buried his head in his hands and let out a groan. Drewry stopped reading.

"My brothers and sisters, let us pray silently," Chase said in a husky voice, never raising his head. "Please pray for me, that the Lord will create in me a clean heart and renew a right spirit within me."

అ

Freetown, Maryland
April 10, 1868

My dear Miss Drewry,
    Please forgive me for not writing sooner. I didn't get your letter until yesterday. Oh, Miss Drewry, your Uncle James just about went clear out of his head when he found out you was gone. He got drunker than a skunk and tore this place up something terrible.
    Why, Miss Drewry, he even took that cane of his and done smash the mirror atop your dresser! And that dresser belonged to your great-great-grandmammy! There be glass everywhere and my Missy done cut her hand real bad trying to clean it up.

gasp, for the view ahead was breathtaking. The long, narrow drive curved gradually left, then right, like a gently flowing river of white crushed stone. Stately magnolia trees lined the entire length of the drive. Pale ivory buds covered each tree, and Drewry anticipated the delightful scent that would perfume the air once the buds burst into blossom.

As Chase slowed the horses, Drewry caught her first glimpse of the house, a mansion more grand than anything she had ever seen. Black shuttered, many-paned windows offset the wide, double doors on the first floor. A dozen tiers of red brick steps led from the drive to the massive portico. Tall columns supported either side of the porch roof, crowned by a second, equally grand porch enclosed by a white picket rail.

A sense of well-being enveloped Drewry as she looked at the four imposing chimneys, silhouetted against the blue, sun-bright sky. Two gigantic, budding oaks flanked the porch. And when Drewry spied the sea of velvety golden daffodils that lined the entire front of the mansion, she smiled down at the children, who had awakened when the horses slowed their gait.

"Daffodils were my mother's favorite flowers," she said to Sally, whose face was pressed against the carriage window.

"Papa says they were my mama's favorite, too." The little girl's voice was soft and subdued.

Drewry grasped the small hand and squeezed it reassuringly. "Perhaps we can gather a big bunch soon. Why, we'll put a bouquet on every windowsill!"

Sally smiled and threw her arms around Drewry's neck. Despite the lie that had brought her here, Drewry was grateful that she could fill the empty spot in this little heart.

⁂

"Well, c'mon in, chile. You must be perishin' with hunger!"

Drewry gasped as she found herself enveloped in the arms of a woman as broad as a carriage, or so it seemed. The force

That ain't the half of it. Then Mr. James, he done took his musket and started waving it at me in the kitchen, real wild like. I throw up my hands and tells him I don't know where you has gone. He say he don't believe me. He wave that musket some more and say he gonna kill me, so I run out the back door to save my skin. He out of his mind, Miss Drewry.

I stay in town for a month, and Missy come to see me. She said Porter Hopkins come looking for you that first day after you gone. He say Mr. James going to pay for pulling a fast one on him. Mr. James say, "Don't worry, Hopkins, you is going to get what you got coming."

Oh, Miss Drewry, don't you even think about coming back to this valley of sorrows. Most the hired hands have left, on account of never being paid. Only four of us left now, including Missy and me. But we can't leave Plumtree Orchards, you know that. This place be our only home.

I am glad you is happy, Miss Drewry, and have found yourself a home, cause this place here ain't no home no more. Mr. James be drunk in the Silver Dollar Saloon most every day, but me and Missy keep things running as best we can.

Pray for us, Miss Drewry. We need the Lord's healing touch if we going to fix Mr. James. Ain't nothing going to be right here at Plumtree Orchards ever again until that man get his heart right with the Lord. He be carrying some mighty heavy burden that only the Good Lord Jesus can lift off of him. Mr. James need to trade in that heavy yoke for the light yoke of Jesus. We be praying for you every day. Amen.

> *Your friend,*
>
> *Jeb*

੨੦

Drewry sighed heavily as she lit the two lanterns in her bed-room. But even the iridescence of their flickering glow failed to lift her spirits.

Grabbing her Bible from the nightstand, she threw herself onto the overstuffed damask chair near the French doors. Outside, the night was black and deep. She lacked the energy even to close the creamy white draperies.

All day long, she had avoided Chase. His strange outburst at their morning devotions continued to haunt her. She longed to reach out to him, to ease whatever was hurting him so badly, but that wasn't possible. She couldn't ask another human be-ing to open his heart to her without responding in kind. She could not listen to his confidences—if, indeed, he would trust her with them—and continue to deceive him. So, she avoided him. She had even excused herself from their evening chat.

Coward! Liar! Miserably, she sank into the comforting embrace of the soft chair and opened her Bible to the morning's psalm—the fifty-first—and found the verse that had struck her so deeply: "Behold, thou desirest truth in the inward parts. . . ."

God desires truth. That was not a new concept. But she had organized her life around *hiding* the truth. Oh, how had she gotten herself into this dilemma? Unable to read further, she flipped forward a few pages, and her eyes fell on the sixth verse of Psalm 55: "Oh that I had wings like a dove! for then would I fly away, and be at rest."

Yes! To be able to fly away. How she would like to do just that. But deep in her heart, she knew fleeing was no answer. Where would she go? What would the children do without her? And what would she do without them . . . and without the hope—however remote—of someday becoming more than

Chase Auburn's nanny . . . The very idea stunned her!

Unable to concentrate on her reading, Drewry shut her Bible, closed her eyes, and tried to pray. But, try as she might, her thoughts rambled and scattered in a thousand directions. She wanted to ask God for help, to beg Him to bring some good of the chaos she'd made of her life. But she didn't believe He was listening—or cared—about her problems. They must seem small indeed to Him who had created all things . . .

All her pleadings for Uncle James had gone unanswered. Her plight had never seemed worse. Surely God had deserted her. How could she trust Him when He seemed so far away and silent?

Drewry must have dozed off, for when she was startled into wakefulness, her neck cramped painfully. The room was filled with an unnaturally bright orange light, and she heard a crackling noise coming from outside.

What was that smell? Smoke?

Leaping to her feet, her Bible falling to the carpeted floor with a dull thud, Drewry ran to the window. A small scream escaped her throat as she covered her mouth with her hand.

Fire! The world was on fire!

eight

Drewry couldn't believe her eyes.

She stood for one terrifying moment, unable to do more than gape at the horror before her. Then she threw open the French doors and rushed out onto the balcony. Heart pounding, she clasped the throat of her high-necked nightdress and stared helplessly at the raging flames. They burned so hot and bright that Drewry could see, despite the lateness of the hour, the sooty gray smoke that roiled above the fiery field.

The world is on fire! The entire horizon glowed red, filling the air near the house with thick clouds of smoke, though the fire was several dozen acres away. She hoped against hope that it wasn't Chase's experimental field . . .

The children! She must go to the children!

Drewry had turned to move back inside, intending to be sure the children were still sleeping peacefully, when she caught sight of Chase, sitting low in the saddle of his big black stallion, galloping full-out toward the blaze. *What can he be thinking!* She gripped the white picket railing that enclosed her balcony. *If he rides into that inferno* . . .

The thought was simply too horrible to contemplate. "Chase!" she shouted, leaning as far over as the rail would allow. "Chase, come back!"

Too late. Already, he was nearly out of sight along the winding path that led from the hired hands' quarters, to the outbuildings, to the pastures and fields beyond the barn. Drewry couldn't tear her eyes from his form, silhouetted against the fire's shimmering brilliance.

Surely he didn't plan to tackle a blaze of such size and magnitude single-handedly! Why, even with the assistance of every hired man on the plantation, the field was as good as gone. Although Drewry had never experienced such a fire before, even she could recognize the truth.

She remembered when Matilda and Claib had told her how grief-stricken Chase had been after Theresa's death. And that he'd come to grips with his anguish only after throwing himself into his plant experiments, facing head-on the obstacles of testing new crops in tobacco-tired soil. He was a man of strength and endurance, to be sure, but even Chase had his limits.

Dozens of times, she had witnessed him in his library—a studious frown lining his handsome brow and a determined gleam in his dark eyes—as he pored over the heavy volumes that lay open on his desk. He'd spared nothing—not time, nor effort, nor money—in setting his plan into motion. But what if this fire cost him everything he'd worked so hard to achieve?

Drewry shuddered involuntarily, thinking of the anguish he must be experiencing as he rode closer, closer to the angry fire's destruction. She was overcome with the need to be with him, to comfort him when he faced the ugly truth that a whole year's work had, quite literally, gone up in smoke.

She ran to her chiffonier and threw open the doors. Grabbing the nearest frock, she slipped out of her nightgown and into the simple, blue cotton dress. She'd barely secured her long, flowing hair with a scrap of ribbon when she heard a soft knock on her door.

"Doo-ree," called a small voice from the hall, "what's that smell?"

"Is it a fire, Drewry?" Sally's tone was edged with anxiety. "Drewry . . . are you awake?"

Immediately, Drewry opened her door and wrapped both children in a hug. "Yes, children," she began, trying to sound calm and reassuring though her heart hammered inside her, "it's a fire."

She was terrified for Chase—not only because of the physical danger he was facing, but because he was emotionally vulnerable, too. But she hid her concern. The children needed to hear some semblance of the truth, of course, or their fears would only escalate, but she must be brave . . . for all of their sakes.

"One of the north fields is burning," she explained.

"Where Papa does his 'sperry-ments'?" Sam asked.

Drewry shrugged. "Possibly."

"Where is he now?" Sally wanted to know.

Drewry sighed. And how was she to answer the child? By telling her that her father had ridden straight into the flames?

She swallowed hard and took a deep breath. Then holding the children at arm's length, she looked them in the eye. "Your father has gone to see if he can put out the fire."

Sam began to cry, and buried his face in Drewry's neck. "He could get burnt up!" he sobbed.

"Hush, now, Sam, darling," she soothed, kissing his soft, round cheek. "Your papa is a brave man. A smart one, too. He won't do anything foolish . . . I—I'm sure of it."

She didn't approve of this half-truth. Not one bit. It was precisely *because* she knew how important the experiments had been to Chase that Drewry's heart continued to thunder. He had told her as recently as last week that he'd invested most of the year's surplus profits in what had, until moments before, thrived in that now-blazing field.

"Will you go to him, Drewry?" Sally asked. "Will you tell him to come back home, where he'll be safe?" The little girl blinked, sending a trail of tears down her rosy cheeks.

Using her thumb, Drewry gently wiped them away. "Yes, children, I'll go," she said softly. "But before I do, you must make me a promise."

Sam and Sally exchanged puzzled glances, then focused on their nanny. "What promise, Drewry?" asked Sally. "We'll do whatever you say."

And they would. Not once in her months at Magnolia Grange had the children deliberately disobeyed Drewry, nor given her cause to scold or punish them. Unlike the "spoiled, bratty offspring of a rich man" that Suzie had described on the Richmond-bound train, Sally and Sam were good children. Sweet-tempered, well-behaved children, who tried diligently to please.

"I want you to promise you'll stay inside with Matilda," she cautioned them. "You're not to go out—not for any reason—until I return." Gently, she placed a hand on each child's cheek. "Do you understand?"

Sam and Sally nodded solemnly.

At that moment, Drewry would have done anything humanly possible to say what they wanted to hear—that their father was safe and would be coming home soon—but she knew better than to give them false hope. Instead, she forced a faint smile.

"What about the water, Drewry?" asked Sally, her eyes round with wonder. "Is there enough water to put out such a big fire?"

Drewry's forefinger, laid over the girl's quivering lips, silenced her. "You're absolutely right, Sally. There isn't enough water on all of Magnolia Grange to put out such a fire. But your father will think of something . . ."

The children began to cry again. "Papa could get hurted," Sam insisted.

Lord, Drewry begged, *guide me . . . Help me find the words to comfort them . . .* It came to her then: "Let's pray, children," she said, pulling them into her arms and speaking the plea that was in her heart.

"Miss Drew, Miss Drew," came an anxious voice, "jus' where do you thinks you is goin'?"

Looking up, Drewry saw Matilda standing in the doorway. "I'm going to look for Chase."

Matilda closed her eyes and folded her hands. "Lawd, Lawd," she prayed aloud, "watch over these bull-headed younguns of

Yourn. Keep Mistah Chase an' Miss Drew safe."

When Matilda opened her eyes, she also opened her arms, and Sally and Sam leapt from Drewry's bed and ran into her motherly embrace. Looking over their shoulders, Matilda said to Drewry, "Well, get on out of heah, then, if you really got a mind to. An' when you find that stubborn man, you tell him this for me: If one hair on his head be singed, I gonna whoop his britches, just like I done when he was a boy."

Nodding, Drewry finished lacing her boots, then slipped past the three, huddled in a teary hug in the hallway, and headed down the stairs.

"And tell him we love him," called Sally as Drewry closed the front door behind her.

❧

At the barn, Drewry was surprised to see Claib leading a saddled horse from the building. "Claib! Just where do you think you're going?"

"Why, goin' to see if I can help Mistah Chase."

Drewry frowned. "You'll do no such thing. If something should happen to Chase, who'd run Magnolia Grange? You're the only one who knows how he'd want things done."

"Ain't nothin' gonna happen to Mistah Chase . . ." Claib said stubbornly. He stuck his booted foot into the stirrup and prepared to swing astride the bay.

"I hope and pray you're right," Drewry said, pulling his foot out of the stirrup. "But what if the unthinkable happens? Who'll watch over Matilda and Bridget? And what about all the hands . . . and their families? No," she insisted, "you're needed here."

Claib stared across the wide expanse of lawn, mesmerized by the fiery horizon. "I s'pose you is right, Miss Drew. But I can't let you go out there alone. Let me get one of the fiel' hands."

Drewry shook off his protest. "I'm sure the others are there already, Claib. And I'm just as sure that not a one of them will be able to talk Chase into coming back here until that fire's completely out. Maybe by the time I get there, the Good Lord will have put the right words into my mouth . . ."

Before the grizzled old man could dissuade her, Drewry climbed into the saddle, slapped the horse's rump, and headed at a full gallop for the burning field.

"You be careful now, Miss Drew!" Claib yelled after her. "Them young uns loves you like a mama. They don't need to be losin' you, too."

Dry and crackling, bright and blinding, the night air grew hotter as Drewry neared the field. Claib was right. The children did love and need her. *Almost as much as I love and need them. Lord,* she prayed, *keep me safe . . . Use me to bless those little ones at home . . .*

Even from this distance, Drewry could see that Chase's men had met him at the burning field. No doubt they had seen the blaze reflected in the night sky and had come to his aid. There would have been almost no time at all to summon them.

Seeing that this was a field of corn that was aflame—not Chase's experimental field—Drewry breathed a quick prayer of thanksgiving. But she must move fast. Already the intensity of the flames were scorching her skin and clothing. Squinting against the brightness, she used the sleeve of her dress to wipe the stinging tears from her eyes.

The men, she could see, had tried to protect themselves against the fire by wrapping their faces in wet neckerchiefs. Furiously, some chopped and hacked around the perimeter of the cornfield, while others raked and hoed, creating a fire break that would keep the flames from spreading to adjacent property.

But it was a windy night, and tiny golden sparks escaped the parent fire. Like unruly children, they rode the summer breeze, settling on a nearby field. Chase's experimental soy crop!

Helpless, Drewry sat in the saddle, hovering near the tree line, coughing and straining to see through the smoky haze. She wanted to help. But what could she do? Would Chase consider her only a bothersome intrusion?

While she was lost in that moment of indecision, the flurry of activity moved south as Chase and his men tried to head off the fire. Weeks ago, to fight the persistent drought that threatened his experiment, Chase had instructed the men to lay mounds of field grass over the soil to protect the delicate roots from the harsh, drying effects of the blazing summer sun.

The thatch had saved the plants.

Now, it could very well mean the end of them!

Dry and parched, the clippings were fuel for the ravenous flames. With a sinking sensation, Drewry knew that the most they could hope for was to keep the fires in these two fields from spreading and destroying any more of Magnolia Grange. *I can't sit idly by a moment longer!* she decided. *I'm going to do what I can!*

Tying her horse to a tree downwind, an acre or two from the fire, Drewry hitched up her skirts and ran toward the field. When she got there, she spied a mattock on the ground. She grabbed it and fell into line alongside Chase's men. Hoisting the heavy tool, she began methodically chopping at the hard, encrusted earth that ringed the fire.

"*Miss* Sheffield!" Chase thundered when he noticed her. "What are you doing out here? And who's minding my children?"

With the back of her hand, Drewry wiped beads of perspiration from her brow and squinted through the thick, roiling smoke. "Matilda, of course," she retorted, stomping over to where he stood, pick-ax in hand. Not once in the months Drewry had been at Magnolia Grange had she seen Chase so angry. But he was furious. Or was it grief that creased that handsome brow?

"Chase," she began, her tone gentler now, "it hasn't rained in weeks, and these fields are as dry as straw. This is a wild-fire. Even *I* know that. Send the men back to their cottages—they've done all they can—and come back to the house with me, where it's safe."

His broad shoulders slumped, as if bowed beneath a great burden, as he looked out across the burning fields.

She took a step closer, and forced him to meet her gaze. "Chase Auburn, you listen to me!" Drewry gestured toward the men, working feverishly to keep the fire at bay. "Someone could be seriously injured. Someone could *die.*" She paused, then continued, "Are these fields worth risking even one life?"

For an instant, he met her eyes, and in that instant, Drewry saw an aching sadness. She started to reach out, to touch him, but he sagged to his knees.

"Gone," he rasped. "All gone. A year of hard work—three years of study before that . . . gone."

He seemed lost in thought. Looking down at him, Drewry was reminded of her helplessness when attempting to console her Uncle James. *Lord,* she prayed, *speak through me. Give Chase, Your servant, peace. Ease his burden . . .*

Tentatively she placed a hand on his shoulder. She longed to say something—anything—to reassure him. But nothing came. No comforting words. No direction. Nothing.

Chase did not even look up. "Go back to the house, Drewry." His tired voice was laced with bitterness. "Go away. Go away and leave me alone. Please."

Her own eyes burned with tears—as much from sadness and rejection as from the smoke and soot. There were tears in his eyes, too. Were these tears caused by the fire . . . by yet another loss . . . or was there something more?

He's ashamed that I've seen him like this, she decided. Drewry couldn't leave him—not now.

With sudden inspiration, she dropped to her knees beside

him. "Oh, Chase," she cried, "I'm so afraid! I can't go back to the house in this state . . . I—I'll frighten the children." She held her breath. It was true, after all. She *was* frightened—for Chase's well-being as well as for her own.

"Won't you pray with me, Chase?" she pleaded. It couldn't hurt anything. Even with no answer to her last desperate plea, she somehow believed that God was watching over them. And without waiting for a reply from Chase, she began asking the Lord for His mercy, for strength to endure whatever came . . .

Chase did not close his eyes, nor did he turn his face toward heaven, as Drewry had done instinctively. Instead, he kept his gaze focused on her—hands folded piously, eyes closed in concentration.

Then, suddenly, as if in answer to her prayer, the skies opened up and a steady rain began to fall. Wonderingly, Chase held out his hand, palm up, and watched as the droplets rolled from his fingertips. The soothing sound of Drewry's prayer blended with the pattering of raindrops on the wide brim of his black felt hat. And mercifully, as she prayed, with every drop of the heavenly liquid, the fields burned with less fury.

He glanced at Drewry in amazement. Her face, illuminated by the fire's fading glow, appeared angelic to him as she knelt there beside him, so lost in prayer that it seemed she was oblivious to the smoldering all around her.

When she concluded her prayer at last, Chase lifted her chin with the tip of his forefinger and stared deep into her eyes. Then, ever so lightly, he kissed her cheek. "Thank you, Drewry, for reminding me that all is not lost. Go back to the house now. I'll be along shortly."

He rose, drawing her to her feet, but she made no move to leave. "If you're staying, I'm staying," she declared, "because . . . well, because you're a—a friend, that's why, and what are friends for, if not to be there in times of trouble?"

Chase sighed deeply, staring across his destroyed fields.

Then, shaking his head, he smiled in resignation. "You are a true friend indeed, Drewry Sheffield, and I wouldn't be surprised if you weren't a messenger of the Lord, too."

If you only knew, she thought, *that I'd like to be so much more than a friend, Chase Auburn . . .*

There! She had admitted it, if only to herself. Such an admission could never be confessed, she knew, not to such a fine and honorable man, whose love for his wife still burned as brightly as the fire that had ravaged these fields only a short time ago. Besides, he deserved better than the likes of Drewry Sheffield, who had stooped to living a lie all these months.

Putting hope behind her, she squared her shoulders. *Well, you may never be his wife, but he has said you are his friend. You'll just have to be satisfied with that.* "Let's go back to the house now, Chase. The children are worried about you . . ."

Chase took a last lingering look at the smoking field before turning his back on it. Then, looking down at Drewry, he asked, "Why did you come out here tonight? Why didn't Claib come, instead?"

"He was ready to leave," she said as they headed for the house, "but I talked him out of it."

Chase frowned. "Claib loves this place every bit as much as I do, and worked on those fields almost as hard as I did. I can't imagine what you could have said to keep him away . . ."

Drewry shrugged. "I simply pointed out that if something happened to you, you'd want him to run Magnolia Grange . . . until you were back on your feet, of course."

"Ahhh, of course," he said, understanding registering in his deep voice. "But why did *you* come, Drewry? Why didn't you send Simon to bring back the news that I was safe?"

Because I had to see for myself, she wanted to say. Instead, she explained, "Because we—that is, the children and Matilda and—and everyone—were worried about you."

A tired smile lifted the corners of his mouth. "But weren't

you afraid . . . of the fire?"

Without a moment's hesitation, she answered him, "I was more afraid of losing you."

He stopped in his tracks and, despite the rain, which was pelting them now, stood looking down at her. Basking in the warmth of his gaze, Drewry's heart raced.

Suddenly, his smile faded, and he brought a damp and sooty wad of paper from his shirt pocket. "I found this tacked to a tree just outside the fire line," he told her, indicating the still smoldering fields with a jerk of his head. "If you're to help me tell Matilda and the children the truth, you'll need to know all the facts."

Frowning, Drewry took the note from him and smoothed it out before reading aloud the words scribbled in haste: "'We warned you not to act like a Yankee! Next time we'll ruin something a lot more valuable than one of your sorry little crop experiments.'"

Her heart was pounding now—with fear. She looked from Chase's scowling face to the scrap of paper still clutched in her hand. "Oh, Chase, it's the Klan again, isn't it?"

"Yes," he hissed, relieving her of the threatening message and jamming it deep into his jacket pocket. "Alden Kelly and his merry band of misfits."

Drewry covered her face with both hands. "Oh, Chase, I'm so sorry," she whimpered. "It's all my fault. If I'd minded my own business that day when he came by . . ."

Unexpectedly, Chase tugged her hands away from her face and stroked her rain-soaked hair. "They didn't do this because of anything you did or said, Drewry," he assured her. "They did it because, despite their repeated threats, I refuse to allow them to intimidate me."

There in the protective circle of his arms, she felt the warmth that radiated from his powerful body. But she also felt his muscles, tensed with concern and anxiety. "They've threatened you before?" she whispered.

Chase nodded. "Nothing as blatant as their midnight visit . . ." He glanced toward the fields. Smoke still billowed above the glow of embers that coated the once-green earth. "Or *this* . . ."

He shook his head sadly. "It's been small things mostly. Snide remarks in town. Dirty looks." He chuckled. "Suddenly I was an outcast when, until recently, my name was clearly part of Richmond's social register."

Their faces were mere inches apart when she looked up at him. "What will we tell the children, Chase?"

"We'll just say that the men in white robes didn't like what I was growing out there. We'll tell everyone to be careful. To stay close to the house. To . . ."

"But wouldn't it be better to pretend it was an accident?" she broke in, "to keep them from worrying unnecessarily?"

His brow furrowed and he backed away. "I'm surprised at you, Miss Sheffield. I thought you and I were of one mind when it came to dealing with the truth." The edge in his voice was chilling.

Drewry remembered their brief conversation that night, alone in the kitchen, after the Klan had paid its frightening midnight visit. Drewry sighed. When she had disembarked from the train in Richmond and allowed Chase to think she was the nanny he'd sent for, she'd promised herself that there would be no other deceptions. *But you're becoming so proficient at lying, it seems the natural thing to do!* she reprimanded herself.

"Of course," she said quietly. "What was I thinking? The truth is always best."

"It's not going to be easy, telling them what happened, of course." Chase took a step nearer and gazed down into her eyes once more. "But it will be easier . . . if you'll be there beside me."

"Oh, Chase, you know I'll be there! Always!" Before she could think what she was doing, she lifted her face, stood on tiptoe, and pressed her lips against his. She kissed him long and hard. To distract him? To comfort him? She didn't know. Nor did she care. She only knew that it felt good and right to be in his arms. To feel his sweet, rain-wet lips on hers.

It ended all too soon. ""I—I'm so sorry!" she stammered breathlessly, stepping away. "I don't know what came over me. I—I only meant to . . ."

Chase pulled her back into his embrace and placed a fingertip over her lips. "Shhh," he whispered. "It's all right. It's been a very long and difficult night for both of us. You only meant to comfort me."

Then, taking her hand to help her over the rutted field, they began walking toward the house. They walked in silence, across the damp lawn, around the circular flowerbed near the drive, up the brick steps, across the marble-floored foyer.

They paused just outside the kitchen, where a light gleamed underneath the door. "You're a remarkable woman, Drewry Sheffield," said Chase. And giving her hand a little squeeze, he released it and thrust open the swinging doors.

"How about a cup of warm milk and some of Matilda's good cookies?" he called cheerfully as he burst into the room. Then, kissing each of his children soundly, Chase added, "Since you're all up anyway, we might as well make a party of it!"

For the moment, the children forgot their fears and giggled at his antics. Over the heads of the children, Matilda and Claib exchanged puzzled glances. Just what was Mistuh Chase up to?

The truth would be told soon enough, his level look conveyed; for now, at least, they would celebrate.

Drewry stood alone, one hand atop each swinging door, peering into the kitchen. *You're a remarkable woman,* he'd said. Her heart swelled with the love she felt for him.

But almost immediately, her elation drained away, much like the air in a child's balloon after it has been punctured. Chase had explained away her kiss as easily as he'd shaken rain from his hat when he entered the house. And he'd reacted to her offer of friendship with kindly deference, not passion. Now she was mortified at the thought of her impetuous gesture . . .

Yes, she loved him. But she didn't deserve a man like Chase Auburn. He was too decent, too good. The most she could ever expect was to be his friend . . . and to love him from afar.

nine

Dear Jeb,

There's so much to tell you, I hardly know where to begin. I have lost many nights' sleep, worrying about you and the others at Plumtree Orchards. I know how difficult Uncle James can be even under the best of circumstances. So my running off and leaving him to deal with Porter Hopkins didn't improve his disposition any, I'm sure. I'm so sorry that my cowardice has put you all at risk. I can only hope that someday you'll be able to forgive me.

This lie I'm living steals my rest, and I must confess that guilt is at the root of those lost hours, as well. I can't tell you how many times I've wanted to confess my sin to Chase. On the one hand, because he's a good-hearted, honest man, he may appreciate my "confession." On the other hand, since he's so decent and honorable, he may despise me for having deceived him at all.

What am I to do, Jeb? Oh, how I miss having you near to advise me. I suppose this suffering is my penance for living as I have these past months.

Please don't worry about me, though. For all my whimpering, I am happy here at Magnolia Grange. It's the weight of the lie that gets me down from time to time, that's all.

Give Missy a hug for me, and be sure to tell
everyone that I send my best. Tell them they're
in my thoughts and prayers each and every day,
and that I miss them all so very much! I miss
you most of all, dear Jeb.

With my deepest affection,
Drewry

੨ৡ

Thanks to the blanket of hay that had been strewn to protect the soy crop from the drought, Drewry soon learned, Chase's experimental field had not been totally destroyed, after all. The soybeans proved to be hardy plants, and very few were devoured by the ravenous flames.

But the clippings caused a problem of an entirely different sort. As the thatch lay, heaped upon the ground, it absorbed the rain like a sponge. And as the days passed and the moisture between the thin blades multiplied, rot set in.

Squatting between the tidy rows, Chase held his hat in one hand and overturned the leaves of one plant with the other. "Fungus!" he spat out. "We have ourselves a raging, spreading fungus here."

Claib knelt beside his boss and inspected the plant. "What we gonna do now, Mistah Chase?"

Chase shook his head glumly. "We're going to pinch off the affected leaves, for starters." Sighing, he rose, shoved his hands into his pockets, and stared at the toes of his dusty boots. "At least, we'll try that first. If it doesn't work, we'll wash and towel the fungus from every single leaf by hand, if we have to!"

"How we gonna make time to do that?" Claib wanted to know. "We got to get set to bring in the other crops, Mistah Chase. Why, if . . ."

Chase frowned. "Where's your faith, man! There's time enough . . . if we don't waste any more of it whimpering!"

"But Mistah Chase," Claib protested, clenching his weathered hat in his hands, "we only got just so many hired hands." He glanced at the field of struggling soy plants and shook his head. "It's gonna take a heap o' time an' help to . . ."

Chase flexed a muscle in his jaw as he replaced his wide-brimmed black felt hat and turned to face his foreman. "It'll get done. We'll see that it does. If we have to work day and night and light this field with lanterns to see what we're doing, we'll get the job done!"

It was Claib's turn to sigh. "If you say so, Mistah Chase." The older man shuffled off toward the barn, muttering under his breath. "Don't see how he plan to save this field and harvest all the rest, though." Claib pulled his hat low on his forehead as he disappeared into the barn.

Chase ignored Claib's negative remarks. *The experiment was working!* he reminded himself. He'd been a gnat's breath away from proving he could make a success of this newfangled plant called the soybean. *If it hadn't been for the Klan's intervention . . .*

But he would *not* allow those lunatic vigilantes to stop him! He'd post guards at all four corners of Magnolia Grange, if need be. He'd arm them with shotguns to protect against another Klan attack.

Drewry's words echoed in his mind: *Is it that important?*

He sighed deeply. The experiment was important, but certainly not worth a man's life . . . not even the life of a Klansman.

Dejected, Chase slumped against the fence that surrounded the barnyard. Chickens clucked around his feet, pecking contentedly at the seeds Matilda had scattered earlier that morning. He was tired. Too tired, even, to shoo them away when they tapped at the toes of his boots. He'd felt much the same weariness the night before, when, on hands and knees, he'd tried in vain to smother the billowing flames with nothing more than an old horse blanket.

"Chase?"

Drewry's voice, like a gentle breeze, reached him. *It's as if she can read my moods,* Chase thought, looking over his shoulder to find the young woman, dressed in a pink frock, headed his way. She looked lovely, with her dark hair falling free around her shoulders that way. She'd tied the top part up, he noticed, with a ribbon the same shade as her dress.

In spite of his somber mood, Chase smiled. "What brings you out here so early in the day?"

"I was chatting with Matilda in the kitchen and saw you out here alone." She fumbled to find the pockets in her dress. "I—I just wondered if there was anything wrong."

Oh, but she was a vision, standing there looking up into his face with those big, dark, luminous eyes of hers. Though she was close enough to touch, he dared not, for fear he'd succumb to the same schoolboyish behavior he'd allowed himself to display last night. She'd only meant to offer him comfort . . . Chase's smile faded.

"Can I get you anything?" she asked. "A glass of lemonade, perhaps?"

"No. Nothing, thank you. I'm about to ride out to the north fields." He glanced toward the back porch, where Matilda was shaking dust from the kitchen doormat. "So tell me, what exciting lessons have you planned for the children today?"

"I thought after they finished their lessons, we'd take a walk and—"

"And *I* thought I'd made it clear that everyone is to stay close to the house," he snapped. Immediately, he regretted his harsh tone as her fresh-faced enthusiasm wilted like a flower in the sun. "I'm sorry," he said with a sigh. "It's just that I'm concerned for your safety—yours and the children's, of course."

"Oh, I only intended to take them as far as the pond," she explained, her eyes downcast. "I thought perhaps we could catch tadpoles, so the children could study how they become frogs."

Chase chuckled in relief. "Of course. How silly of me not to trust you. I know you have my children's best interests at heart."

He wanted to say more. So much more. He wanted to tell her how lovely she looked in her plain pink dress. He wanted to tell her how ridiculous he felt for jumping to conclusions. He wanted to tell her she had the biggest, brownest eyes he'd ever seen, and the sweetest, softest lips . . .

Chase cleared his throat, removed his hat, and slid its brim, between thumb and forefinger, round and round. He wanted to tell her how sorry he was for the way he'd behaved last night. He suspected she'd seen him blubbering like a babe. And that kiss . . . How he regretted surrendering to that kiss! Taking advantage of a young woman as sweet and innocent as Drewry when she'd only intended to offer him a bit of comfort in his time of need! *Forgive me for my display of weakness last night,* he wanted to say. Chase closed his eyes for a long moment and added, *and forgive me, my darling Theresa, for betraying your memory in the arms of another woman.*

"Well," she said in a small voice, glancing toward the house, "I'll just fetch the children, then, and we'll be on our way to the pond. . . ."

First, he'd frightened her with his harsh accusation, Chase thought miserably. And now he'd made her uncomfortable with his hemming and hawing. He would have given anything to start the conversation over again.

"Matilda will protest at first, but I'm sure you can convince her to let you borrow a few canning jars for the project." Chase gave her a wink and, without even thinking, reached out and tenderly touched her cheek.

Drewry's smile widened, he noticed, and that gentle, loving light returned to her eyes. "She *is* more bark than bite, isn't she?"

Chase blinked. "Oh . . . Matilda, you mean," he said distractedly. "Yes. All bark and no bite."

Drewry took a step back, turned, and headed for the kitchen. "Matilda says she's fixing ham and pea soup for lunch," she called to him from the bottom step of the porch. "Perhaps I'll ride out with some when it's ready."

With that, she stepped into the kitchen and closed the screen door quietly behind her.

Chase stood, his hand extended as it had been when he'd touched her cheek. *She's out of your reach,* he told himself. *Completely out of your reach. And that's the way it should stay.*

⁂

Drewry shifted uneasily on the old oak pew. No matter how hard she tried to concentrate, her thoughts kept drifting from the worship service. Her conscience stung as painfully as when she pricked her finger on a blackberry bramble.

She peeked at the faces of the people sitting nearby, their heads reverently bowed. Each seemed intent on the minister's prayers of intercession. Drewry smiled, recalling how warmly the good people of Calvary Church had welcomed her as one of their own. Over the summer, she'd come to know them and to look forward to their conversations at the socials after Sunday school and church.

They had accepted her as part of the Auburn family. In fact, Drewry often wondered if several of the ladies of the missionary society hadn't already pegged her for the next Mrs. Auburn. To the casual observer, she supposed that she, Chase, and the children—sitting together in the Auburn pew—did resemble any one of the congenial young families that comprised the congregation of this country church.

She had been accepted without question and without reservation. And therein lay the source of her prickly conscience. *Oh, Lord, I know it's wrong to keep up this deceit, but I'm so far in now, I don't know how to get myself out.*

Just as often as Drewry had considered confessing her cha-rade to Chase, she had changed her mind. These people seemed to love her, but they loved her because they believed her to be something she was *not*. If they discovered the real Drewry Sheffield, she reasoned, they'd cast her away as easily as Uncle James had.

The services at Calvary—inspiring sermons and enthusias-tically sung hymns—reminded Drewry of her church back home in Freetown. The Sheffields, too, had had their own pew, and in those early years, she'd sat wedged between her mama and papa. After their deaths, Uncle James had sat beside her. When he stopped attending services, she'd sat alone. How wonder-ful it was to be included in a family again, a family she could call her own . . . at least until her secret was discovered.

She let out a trembling sigh, which drew a concerned look from Chase.

"Is everything all right?" he mouthed.

Over the heads of the children, she smiled reassuringly and nodded, wishing she could truly open her heart to Chase and tell him the whole ugly truth. But that was quite out of the question. She couldn't risk being abandoned again. Surely God, if He were as understanding and compassionate as she hoped He was, would not expect such an impossible thing of her.

Practically the entire congregation had come to church that morning, Drewry guessed as she glanced again around the crowded sanctuary. Young boys, mimicking the behavior of their farmer fathers, sat stiffly in their Sunday suits, clutching their hats, while the women and girls perched on the pews in their best frocks, bedecked with ribbons and lace in a bouquet of summer colors.

The swish of fans filled the humid air. From the corner of her eye, Drewry saw that even Chase was fanning himself, the pink shell-shaped fan looking ridiculous in his big, tanned hands. She smiled secretly. Only a man sure of his manhood could use a lady's fan without embarrassment, she thought. But then, Chase's confidence was just one of the many things she cherished about him.

Sally passed Drewry one of the paper fans provided by the usher. "You look all hot, Drewry," she whispered loudly, looking herself like a cherub in her yellow straw bonnet encircled with a halo of pink roses.

Drewry patted the girl's hand and pretended to be paying attention to every word of Pastor Tillman's sermon. *I'm hot, all right,* she thought angrily. *Hot under the collar of all this Sunday finery! I have a home now. Respect. Affection. I'll not risk it all just to ease my conscience!*

"As faithful Christians," Pastor Tillman was saying, "we do the right thing . . . not so much because we fear God's punishment, but because this is how we show the world that we are imitating the life of our Lord, Jesus Christ."

Drewry gasped. It was as if the pastor had read her mind!

"We must strive to mature as Christians," he continued. "To grow up, not just in body, but in spirit . . ."

She considered his words a moment longer. Then, defiantly, Drewry sat up straighter and squared her shoulders. She folded her white-gloved hands over the fan in her lap and lifted her chin. *If a guilty conscience is the price for my happy life at Magnolia Grange, so be it! I'll just have to learn to live with it!*

&

Chase closed his eyes and tried in vain to focus on the sermon. Only moments before, Drewry had told him with that polite nod of her head that all was well. But he didn't believe her for an instant. He had eyes, after all. He could see that something was definitely wrong. That sigh . . . it sounded as if the weight of the Confederacy rested on her slender shoulders.

Yes, indeed, Miss Drewry Sheffield, as much as you may

deny it, there's something terribly amiss in your life. Just as there's something amiss in mine . . .

The memory of Drewry's sudden, impassioned kiss flooded his mind. His temples pounded as he recalled the way her lips had felt against his.

Her boldness had taken him by surprise, to be sure, but as his arms had instinctively closed around her, kissing her had seemed the most natural thing in the world. And wasn't her no-nonsense boldness one of the qualities he admired most about her?

He remembered the raw hurt that glittered in her dark eyes when he'd pulled away from their embrace and held her at arm's length. He hadn't said a word. But something told him she'd read his silence as bald-faced rejection.

The conflict that tore at his soul was almost like physical pain. He had wanted to gather Drewry to him and declare his undying love, and yet, how could he? He'd promised that love to Theresa. Besides, he didn't dare risk loving like that again. It simply hurt too much when it was gone . . .

Opening his eyes, he caught Drewry shifting on the hard bench. *How thoughtless of you, Chase Auburn. You should have brought a cushion for her and the children. You know Pastor Tillman is not known for the brevity of his sermons.*

He noticed Drewry patting his daughter's hand after accepting one of those contraptions they called fans. He smiled. Already, the children treated her more like a mother than a nanny. How quickly the web of love had woven those three together!

Could he dare allow himself to be part of that silken web? Would she even want him . . . after his strange outburst at morning devotions the other day? Her kiss seemed to promise that she would . . .

Almost unconsciously, Chase's hand sought the ferrotype of his wife, hidden in the pocket of his coat. There was no need to take it out and examine it, for her likeness was etched in his mind. His lovely Theresa, with her long dark hair, her coal-black eyes, her wistful smile . . . She had died giving him Sam. How could he betray her!

Overwhelmed with emotion, Chase closed his eyes again. He remembered his wife the last time he'd seen her alive, her skin as waxen white as the pillowslip upon which she lay. It had broken his heart to hear her words then, and they came back to him now with a fresh pang of grief: "You must re-marry, Chase," she'd said, her voice thin and labored. "I don't want you and the children to be alone. The Lord will bring you a new love . . ."

He had stared blankly at her, twining a strand of her dark hair round his finger. Words had deserted him, just as they'd deserted him in the field with Drewry.

He didn't *want* a new love. His fingers tightened around the handle of the fan he held, almost snapping the fragile wood in two. Fear and guilt—his two crusty old friends. Far easier to live with these two than to face the unknown territory of new love.

"You is as stubborn a man as I ever knowed," Matilda had chastised earlier that week. "Come in here all down in the dumps, sayin' you don't know why . . ."

"But I'm fine," he'd defended. "I'm not . . ."

"Mistah Chase, I been lookin' into them eyes of yourn ever since I powdered your li'l round bottom. Don't tell me you's fine, 'cause I know perfectly well you ain't."

Chase knew better than to argue with Matilda. He had perched on a high stool and stared sullenly, silently, into the mug of coffee she had poured him.

"I'll tell you why you look so sorrowful. You is afraid of Miss Drew, that's what!"

His head snapped up at her remark. "Afraid of her! Why, that's rubbish!"

She wagged a plump finger under his nose. "Now, I's not sayin' you ain't a brave man, Mistah Chase. You wasn't afeared of teachin' your slaves to read an' write. And you wasn't afeared of steppin' out and provin' you could grow more than tobaccy and cotton out yonder. An' you didn't let folks in town keep you from openin' the first hothouse in these parts.

"Yet you be afraid to admit how you feel 'bout Miss Drewry." She threw up her hands. "I declare, I don't know what I'm gonna do with you!"

He'd remained silent, both hands wrapped tightly around the big white coffee mug, knowing she hadn't finished her tongue-lashing yet.

"You think Miss T'resa want you to be unhappy? I was there when she died, and don't you forget it. I heerd what she say to you at the end."

Chase took a deep breath. *Where's your courage, man! What if Drewry, even with her secret past, is the woman Theresa prayed God would bring into your life? Who are you to go against the will of God!*

As Pastor Tillman wound up his sermon, Chase kept his eyes closed. Deep within himself, he found that quiet spot of resignation, where he stood before his Creator and admitted that he was not the master of his own fate. He hadn't been the master of his fate for many years—not since the day he'd renewed his commitment to Christ as a young man in this very church.

He shook his head. *Thy will be done, Lord,* he prayed. *Thy will be done.*

When Chase opened his eyes, he found Drewry studying him. She blushed to her hair roots, he noticed, before quickly turning away.

ten

Dear Miss Drew,

I read your letter to Missy, and she say to tell
you she loves you and is praying for you. She
say don't worry 'bout us here at Plumtree
Orchards, 'cause your uncle is quieter these
days. Maybe, the Good Lord is gonna answer
our prayers and set this man free from his
demons.

I understand why you feel bad about telling
that lie, Miss Drew. Nobody blames you for
telling it, least of all, sweet Jesus. What could
you do but leave this place? Not a one of us
wanted to see you married to old Porter
Hopkins!

You was brung up to live by God's law. Now
you just ain't used to telling lies. So nothing will
make you feel better, excepting the truth.

Go to Mr. Chase and tell him. If he be as
kind and honorable as you say, he will understand. He will remember all the good you been
doing for his children, and the many times you
give him kind words, too. Even if the truth make
him angry, you got to tell it. "The truth shall set
you free" say the Good Book. You ain't going to
feel right again till everything is out in the open.

Sound to me like you love this man, Miss
Drew. Missy say to tell you to "build on a strong
foundation," like the Bible say. Start on the

> *right foot.*
> *We be praying for you, like always.*
>> *Your good friend,*
>>> *Jeb*

Drewry held the letter in her hands and wept, glad she'd had the foresight to close her door before opening the envelope. She knew Jeb was right. For as long as she could remember, she'd started each day reciting John 13:15: "For I have given you an example, that ye should do as I have done to you." And for as long as she could remember, she'd been living by that Golden Rule.

Until coming to Magnolia Grange . . .

Drewry replaced Jeb's letter in the envelope and sat back in the rose-colored damask morning seat. Christ would not have lied to anyone as she had lied to Chase. He would not have lived a life of deception, as she had. She knew that if she was ever to begin trying to pattern her life after the Lord's, she must tell Chase everything, as Jeb had suggested.

But Drewry wondered if she possessed enough inner strength to tell him the whole truth. She would need mountains of spiritual strength to live with his disapproval . . . and possible rejection.

She crossed the room and sat at her desk. Grasping the brass drawer pull, she heard the quiet protest of the wood as she eased out the drawer. Withdrawing a sheet of creamy vellum, she placed it on the forest-green desk blotter. The quill's tip clinked quietly against the tiny glass jar as she carefully dipped it into the ink:

> *Dear Jeb,*
>> *I have received your latest letter, and I assure you, I have taken your good advice to heart.*
>> *It pleases me to hear that Uncle James has*

*been behaving more like his old self of late. You
can be sure that I'll continue to pray for his
healing!*

*And I beseech your continued prayers, too, as
some very peculiar things have been going on
around here. Matilda says the things I've been
hearing and smelling are caused by ghosts! She
is a spirited old thing and enjoys seeing my
stunned reaction to her stories. But, seriously,
there is no rational explanation for what has
been going on in the middle of the night.*

*I can't tell you how many times I've stood on
my balcony, overlooking the lawn, and caught
the scent of a cigar. I've heard muffled voices,
too, and, occasionally, what sounds like a man's
cough. But it's the sound of wicked laughter that
tells me that the Klan has been keeping an eye
on us here at Magnolia Grange for quite some
time. I fear that burning Chase's experimental
field was only the first of many horrible sur-
prises they have in store for us if he doesn't give
in to their demands.*

*I didn't mention the fire to worry you, Jeb, for
we are all well. I mention it only because it is
the reason I cannot yet tell Chase the truth. So
for now, at least, while he has so much on his
mind, I'll keep my dreadful secret.*

*Remember that I think of you often and pray
for you always. Give my love to Missy and the
others.*

Fondly,
Drewry

It's all well and good for Jeb to preach honesty, but he's not—

nor has he ever been—in a situation like this! Drewry impatiently snapped the pink linen cloth across the long table in preparation for Sally's birthday party.

"What's wrong wid you, Miss Drew?" Matilda asked from across the dining room, where she was decorating the sideboard with gaily colored paper streamers and big yellow letters that spelled out "Happy Birthday, Sally."

"It's nothing, Matilda." Drewry smoothed the cloth with her hands, then stepped back to eye the effect. "I'm just tired, I guess."

"You is more than tired. You been like a cat on a hot tin roof these days. I been watchin' you. Somethin' troublin' you, missy, an' I knows it!" the housekeeper mumbled on her way to the kitchen to bring in a tempting array of party foods.

Drewry sighed and straightened. She ignored Matilda's comments and busied herself with an arrangement of fresh-picked purple grapes and butter cookies on a three-tiered silver cake stand.

"When we're finished, maybe I'll take a nap with the children," Drewry said nonchalantly. "I'll have plenty of time, since the guests aren't to arrive until four-thirty."

In the process of trying to balance a dozen little cakes, dusted with red sugar sand, on the top tier, her hand slipped. Before she knew it, the whole stand toppled, sending grapes and cakes cascading down onto little sandwiches and petits fours.

Frantically, Drewry reached out to right the stand, but succeeded only in knocking over the cut glass pitcher of lemonade, the contents of which flooded the table and dripped onto the hardwood floor.

"Oh, no! Even Sally's birthday cake has been splashed with lemonade!" Drewry groaned, putting her hands to her face and bursting into tears.

Matilda was at her side in an instant. "There, there, honey lamb," she whispered, wrapping Drewry in a massive hug.

"You just hush now and come with me."

Drewry allowed herself to be led to the white wicker settee on the porch.

"Don't you worry none," Matilda soothed, patting her shoulder. "There's plenty more food where that come from. It's you I's worried 'bout."

The compassionate tone of Matilda's voice, along with her reassuring hug, inspired fresh sobs from Drewry.

"I think I knows what's botherin' you, Miss Drew."

How could she know? Drewry wondered. *How could she know, and still treat me with such kindness?*

Matilda pulled an envelope from her apron pocket. "This was with the rest of the mail I c'lected from the post office las' week," she explained, handing it to Drewry. "It's addressed to Mistah Chase, I know, but it be part of my job to get the household bills ready for him to pay. I always opens his mail."

Drewry slid the letter from its official-looking envelope. The moment her eyes fell on the letterhead—"Wheatley Employment Agency, Baltimore, Maryland"—her heart sank. Alarmed, she met Matilda's knowing look.

"It say a gal name of Suzie was to arrive on the train from Baltimore."

Drewry nodded. "I was her seatmate all the way to Richmond."

"You gonna tell ole Matilda about it?" The twinkle in her eyes told Drewry she was safe.

Drewry blotted her tears and blew her nose on her starched white hanky. Within moments, it seemed, she had spilled the whole ugly story.

"Mmmm." Matilda nodded sagely. "You'd best tell Mistah Chase, soon as you can."

Drewry shook her head. "I can't. Not yet."

"Why not, chile? The man love you. You mark my words: 'The truth shall set you free,'" she quoted.

Drewry's tears started again in earnest. "He won't understand; he can't possibly understand. He's too good. Too decent. Too honest . . ."

"Lay this problem at the feet of Jesus, honey lamb. Whatever ails you, take it to Him."

Drewry pulled away from Matilda's touch. "What's the use?" she shot back. "God has never answered my prayers before. Well, hardly ever," she amended, remembering the night of the drought-breaking rain. "When I was an orphan, I begged Him to bring my mama and my papa back. And then, when Uncle James kept getting worse . . ."

Drewry found herself enclosed in another bear hug. For several moments, Matilda hummed softly, rocking her back and forth as if she were a distraught child. Drewry relaxed into the motherly embrace and found herself comforted. It occurred to her that even though Matilda knew the whole awful truth about her, she loved her still.

The older woman pointed to the cloudless blue sky. "You see them stars, Miss Drewry?"

Drewry couldn't help giggling. "Of course not. It's broad daylight!"

"Oh, but the stars are up there, honey lamb. I read it in a book onct. The Lord God put them stars up in the sky, and they're there day an' night. Only, in the daytime, we can't see 'em, on account of the brightness of the sun."

Drewry waited patiently, wondering where Matilda's discourse was leading.

"Sometimes, in the dark o' night, a shootin' star will suddenly come into view, and we may think it just 'peared out of nowhere. But it was really there all along."

Drewry looked heavenward, at the sky filled with hidden stars.

"Don't you see, chile? It's like you, lookin' for answers to your prayers. God don't always answer with a yes or a no. Sometimes, His answer be *no answer a'tall.*

"You be like a chile, Miss Drew, who don't b'lieve they is stars, jus' 'cause you can't see 'em in the daytime."

Despite the heat of the day, a chill crept down Drewry's back. *Matilda is absolutely right. Why haven't I realized it before!*

"The answers to your prayers are like them stars," the woman said softly. "They always there, whether you see 'em or not. God is like that, honey pie. He always answer your prayers. Mebbe not like you want Him to, but He always do what He know is best for you."

Drewry brushed the last of the tears from her cheeks. "Thank you, Matilda," she said, "for teaching me to look for the hidden stars. I've been behaving like a spoiled little girl all my life, demanding proof that God loves me."

She stood to her feet decisively and announced, "I think it's high time for me to grow up!"

&

A bevy of little girls in party dresses and boys in sailor suits milled about in the front parlor, balancing teacups and plates of finger foods like miniature adults. Some made strained, polite conversation, while others sat quietly, listening to the violin quartet that filled the house with the soft music of Mozart.

Little Sally, resplendent in the blue dress Drewry had made for her, played the part of the model hostess with apparent ease. As instructed by Drewry, she curtsied to the parents of each child, never tugged at her white gloves, and placed each gaily wrapped gift on the table without appearing too eager to rip it open.

Drewry had to suppress a laugh at the children's earnest good manners, knowing well how impatient they were to get to the fun and games. Even Sam was behaving like a dignified little gentleman.

But learning gentle manners was a requirement for Chase's children, and as their nanny, part of Drewry's job was to see that they received the training that would carry them into adulthood. Now she realized it was also her job to grow into the full maturity of womanhood herself. Thanks to Matilda, she could now trust God to see her through . . . once she had come clean with Chase.

"There's nothing quite so innocent and full of promise as a little girl's birthday party, is there?"

Chase's deep voice interrupted Drewry's musings. She turned to find herself looking up into his sober gaze. He appeared strained, his chiseled features taut with some unknown burden. Despite the lines of fatigue etched on his face, he appeared the consummate master of Magnolia Grange—his flawlessly tailored black jacket hugging broad shoulders, erect with an air of authority. He was a man accustomed to being in command, she reminded herself, accustomed to respect . . . not deceit.

I must tell him, Drewry resolved. Remembering Pastor Tillman's sermon and Matilda's wise counsel, she knew it was the right thing, the *only* thing to do. But she found the prospect of confession frightening. Found his thoroughly masculine presence unnerving as well.

Thinking of his touch the night she had so shamelessly thrown herself into his arms, Drewry felt a quickening pulse throbbing in the hollow of her throat. *Whatever possessed you?* she scolded herself. *What must he think of you now?*

She dragged her gaze from his and focused her attention on Sally, playing hostess only a few feet away.

"Is something wrong, Drewry?" he asked kindly. "Is there anything I can do for you?"

Even his voice stirred her senses. "N—no. Well, not exactly. But all the same, I'd like a few moments alone with you, Chase." She forced her voice to remain firm, despite her quivering nerves. Her mind raced. How would she find the words? And how would she handle his obvious disappointment in her? Would he tell her to pack up and leave immediately? If so, where would she go?

"Would the porch be a convenient place?"

"Hmmm?" She started from her reverie. "Oh . . . yes, of course. The porch would be just fine."

Chase lightly held her elbow as he steered her across the room, crowded with children. Even his touch was disturbing. Drewry forced herself to smile and send a reassuring wave to Sally. The child nodded, beaming.

"This party is just what she needed," Drewry said to Chase as they settled onto the same wicker settee where, only an hour or two ago, she had made her confession to Matilda.

"Yes, our little Sally is becoming quite the poised young lady . . . thanks to you, I might add." His approving gaze swept her from head to toe. "By the way, Miss Sheffield, did I tell you how lovely you look today? Green becomes you."

The deep timbre of his voice sent a delicious shiver down Drewry's spine. "How thoughtful of you to say so. A woman appreciates a man who notices such things." Again, she couldn't believe she'd been so bold. Whatever was she doing?

Suddenly, their gazes locked. Somewhere nearby, a bird chirped. The scent of roses, mingled with newmown grass, lay heavy on the humid afternoon air. A feathery wind riffled the leaves on the trees and played in her hair, reminding her again of Chase's gentle touch.

Drewry found herself admiring the firm set of his jaw, and longed to reach over and lightly trace the outline of it with her fingertips. She trembled slightly at the memory of how he had crushed her to his chest, how her hands had curled so willingly around those strong shoulders.

But this was no time for idle daydreams. She shook her head to clear it, then returned to the matter at hand. *I can't live with this deception any longer. I must be honest with him, once and for all. And if I must, why not now?*

Drewry took a deep breath, squared her shoulders, and

plunged in. "Chase . . . there is something I must tell you . . . a confession, really. . . ."

"Papa! Papa!" shouted Sally. Tears streaming down her face, the little girl ran across the terrace toward her father, who leapt to his feet at the first sounds of her distress.

"Sweetheart, what is it?" He dropped onto one knee and gathered her close as the child sobbed convulsively.

"Oh, Papa. They're so mean!"

"Who is mean, sweetheart?"

"Nellie and Cornelia." Sally hiccupped. "They said their daddies call you names. They say you're not a good Virginian. They say you're—you're crazy!"

Chase grinned broadly and whipped out his handkerchief. "Now, now, sweetheart. Don't cry."

"They say you treat blacks like reg'lar folks," she said as he dabbed at her tears.

"Well, Miss Sally Ann Auburn, can you tell me *why* I treat blacks like reg'lar folks?"

Sally blinked and met his eyes. "'Cause all people are God's children, made in His image. So, we must treat every single person with respect."

Chase smiled. "That's my girl! *You* know what's right. Now, when people think or say cruel things—does that change the truth?"

Sally shook her head. "No, Papa."

Tenderly, Chase pushed an errant curl out of his daughter's eyes. "Then don't ever let anyone make you doubt what's right. Living with integrity is the only way to please the Lord."

"Yes, Papa." Sally looked adoringly at her father, then furrowed her brow in a look of puzzlement. "Papa, what does *in-teg-ri-ty* mean?"

Chase chuckled. "It means honesty, sweetheart. Honesty and purity of heart."

Sally brightened. Stretching on tiptoe to give him a hug,

she skipped gaily back to her party.

Chase stood to his full, towering height, putting Drewry in mind of the spruce trees that lined the western edge of the property. "She's learning fast," he observed.

"Yes." Drewry squirmed uncomfortably in her seat and rose to stand beside him. "Perhaps we should get back. . . ."

"Yes. I'm scheduled to referee a croquet game on the lawn once the birthday girl cuts her cake." He turned to leave the terrace, then stopped abruptly. "But wait—didn't you have something important to tell me? A confession, I believe you called it?"

Drewry wondered if he could hear the mad beating of her heart. She clasped her hands together, wishing for a way to forestall the inevitable. But how would she tell him now, especially after the touching scene she had just witnessed? "I—I just wanted to tell you . . . to confess . . ."

The way he stood there, grinning at her, took Drewry's breath. She began again. "I just wanted to confess how . . . *happy* . . . I am here, Chase." She swallowed her cowardice like bitter bile. A heavy sense of foreboding fell over her. Integrity in her own life was seriously lacking. And she wasn't about to confess that lack to this man who prized the virtue so highly!

Chase hesitated for a moment, as if waiting to hear more. But Drewry kept quiet. Silently she watched the sunshine filtering through a cloud, carving the planes of his face into interesting angles. Her heart sank. How much longer could she go on playing this game—with him *and* with God?

"I'm glad to hear that, Drewry." Gallantly Chase extended his elbow. "Now, shall we rejoin the party?"

As she tucked her arm into his and walked back into the house, she glanced up at the sky. Somewhere up there, behind that clear blue canvas, the stars twinkled chastely.

She couldn't help wondering, though, how they managed to stay so completely hidden from view.

eleven

Dear Miss Drew,

What a wonderful surprise to get another letter from you so soon. Missy and me read it three, four times over.

Things sound mighty exciting down in Richmond, that's for sure. And things here in Freetown is mighty exciting, too. Your uncle and me had us a big clash, Miss Drew. He went into town last week, and decide to stop in at the post office to get the mail. He come home from town with the packages and the envelopes, bellowing like a bull. He call me a sneaky snake. Ask me how could I keep your whereabouts a secret, knowing how he be suffering over missing you. Can't tell you where Miss Drew is, I tell him, cause I promise not to. She be scared, I say, that you gonna make her marry old Porter Hopkins.

Mr. James get real quiet. Sit in his big leather chair and start to weep. He say you mean everything to him, Miss Drew, since you be practically the only family he got left in all the world. Then he say he gonna quit drinking whiskey. Going to quit gambling, too. I believe it when I see it, I say to myself. Well, it been nearly two weeks now, and Mr. James ain't touched a drop of whiskey in all this time. Ain't played no cards, neither, far as I can tell.

Maybe this change be on account of Miss

Naomi. Her daddy be the minister over on the
Piscataway reservation. Her mama be a
Susquehannock Indian, Mr. James tell me. I
ain't seen Miss Naomi yet, but your uncle say
she more beautiful than a sunrise. He say she
have hair the color of the midnight sky and eyes
as brown as roasted chestnuts. He say me and
Miss Naomi has lots in common, since we both
half-breeds.

Mr. James, he go to Sunday services and read
his Bible every night before bed. Why, he even
say a word of thanks before meals, just like we
done before the War. Things be about as right as
right can get round here, Miss Drew. All this
time, I offer up my humble prayers that the Lord
would see fit to put the heart and soul back into
Mr. James, and though I believed it would
happen, I reckoned I'd be long gone before that
day come. But praise God, He let me witness the
change with my very own eyes!

So don't you worry none about us, Miss Drew.
Mr. James say to tell you he loves you, and that
he is sorry for all the grief he cause you. He
wants to find a way to say so in person, cause he
don't want to start his new life with Miss Naomi
till he sets right all the things he done wrong.
I'll wait to hear from you, Miss Drew.

Look like you got lots of hard decisions to
make. Telling the whole truth to Mr. Chase and
forgiving your uncle ain't gonna be easy. But if
the Lord can help your uncle do the right thing,
he can sure help you.

Missy and me gonna keep praying for you.
And we thank you for your prayers, too. Seems

they done a lot of good!

> *Your friend,*
> *Jeb*

Drewry sat, stunned into silence, Jeb's letter in her trembling hands.

So Uncle James wanted a reconciliation. Drewry didn't know if she had the strength of character to forgive him. It would be wonderful, she acknowledged, to have him in her life again. Especially if, as Jeb had written, he had truly given up whiskey and gambling.

But Drewry wondered about the woman in Uncle James's life. He'd always been a ladies' man. But not once could she recall a woman he'd been willing to change his habits for—a woman he was willing to make a commitment to. This teacher of the Indians must be special, indeed, if he'd even gone back to church for her!

Mr. James, he say yóu mean everything to him, Drewry read again, *and he wants to find a way to tell you in person how sorry he be for all the grief he cause you.*

Drewry's heart beat faster at the thought of Uncle James coming to Richmond. How would she arrange for such a meeting? And how would she explain it to Chase?

Sighing, she carefully tucked Jeb's letter into the wide, curved drawer of her desk. Resting her elbows on its shining surface, Drewry held her head in her hands and closed her eyes. *Why must life be so complicated?*

ૐ

The children were asleep in their rooms, taking their afternoon naps, when Drewry, with no duties to perform, wandered down to the kitchen. Maybe she could help Matilda with dinner.

The woman's white teeth gleamed in the broad black face as she handed Drewry a small metal bucket. "Go on down the path yonder," Matilda said, "an' pick me this pail full of black-berries. I'm just about to roll out some dough to make a black-berry pie for dessert."

It would be wonderful to be outdoors—alone—to contem-plate the state of her confusing life, Drewry decided. She hitched up the hem of her gray cotton dress and tucked it into the belt at her waist to protect the white lace trim from gather-ing dust and dirt along the path. And because it was warmer outside than she'd expected when she'd put on the high-col-lared frock, she undid the velvet-covered button at the neck-line. Thankfully, she'd wound her hair into a bun and tucked it into a lacy white chignon.

The gentle July breeze cooled her bare neck as she stepped lightly down the beaten path. Jeb's earlier advice—to tell Chase the truth about herself—confirmed Matilda's sentiments be-fore Sally's party about honesty. And Drewry would have con-fessed, too, if not for Sally's tearful interruption.

Drewry inhaled sharply. *No telling where you'd be right now if you'd gone ahead with it!* Still, it was the right thing to do, and she knew it. *Well, you can tell him later. After he's fully recuperated from the fire . . .*

The path narrowed as the willowy blackberry branches, bowed under their sweet burden, hung low. For several dozen yards, she plucked the near-black, shining berries and dropped them into the silvery bucket, popping one of the sweet-sour treats into her mouth for every five that hit the bucket's bot-tom.

She had almost reached the clearing at the far end of the path when she noticed it. Matilda had told her that a tiny, rough-hewn chapel sat in the middle of a meadow, but since she'd never traveled this far down the path before, Drewry had never seen it for herself. The peaked roof, shingled with weath-ered shakes, and the whitewashed half-walls that supported it, glowed warmly in the afternoon sun.

The small building seemed to beckon to her. Leaving the path, she made her way to the door. Inside, where it was cool and shady, two rows of wooden benches lined the earthen floor. Up front, she saw an altar of split rail construction, and high above it, a crude wooden cross, fashioned from sturdy oak branches.

Drewry took a seat on the aisle and tried to picture the chapel the way Matilda had described it, decorated with yellow satin bows and bouquets of roses, grown in Chase's hothouse, for the Easter sunrise service. She blinked, and imagined it bedecked with holly and boxwood and crimson poinsettias during the Christmas season.

Near the front of the chapel, running the length of the altar, Drewry noticed the kneeler. She placed her half-filled bucket of berries on the bench and walked purposefully toward it. Then, lifting her skirts, she knelt.

Take your problems to Jesus, honey lamb, Matilda had said. Folding her hands, Drewry looked up at the cross. "I do not wish to be a deceiver," she prayed earnestly. "Lord, I want nothing more than to confess this horrible sin and beg Chase's forgiveness."

Tears welled up in Drewry's eyes and a sob ached in her throat. *Help me find the strength to do what is right,* she prayed silently. *Give me the wisdom to know when the time is right to tell the truth.*

In the moments of silence that followed, Drewry experienced a calming of her spirit she had never known before. She felt certain that this peace was the Lord's way of telling her that He would show her when and where to make her full confession.

Pleased with her decision to follow God's leading, she stood, grabbed her berry bucket, and headed for the path that led back to the manor house. Halfway there, as she picked more berries, Drewry thought she heard a masculine sound—as if someone were clearing his throat—somewhere to the north of the path.

She parted the low-growing foliage to peer into the field beyond, and saw Chase standing alone in the middle of the flower-filled meadow. Because he seemed so deep in thought, Drewry was concerned that her sudden appearance might startle him. Besides, he looked so forlorn that he was sure to be embarrassed if she joined him without warning.

Quietly, Drewry backed up a few steps, then made her way forward again, making as much noise as possible.

"Who's there?" he called.

"It's Drewry." Only then did she allow him to see her peeking through the bushes. "Chase, what are you doing way out here?"

In a few long strides, he was beside her on the path, beneath a canopy of pine, maple, and birch branches. "I was asking the Lord's guidance in finding a new field to test my plants," he said, smiling. "And what brings *you* all this way from the house?"

Drewry held her bucket out for him to see. "As Sam might say, I'm on a *berry* important mission—dessert!"

Chase threw back his head and laughed heartily. "Well, I'm 'berry' impressed."

The music of his laughter echoed through the meadow. "I can't recall the last time I've done a thing like this," he admitted, wiping away the tears of release.

Drewry feigned hurt feelings. "You find me amusing, Mr. Auburn?"

He met her gaze, his smile fading. "I find you . . . irresistible," he breathed. Suddenly, with no warning whatsoever, he pulled her close. "You smell like lilacs," he sighed into her ear.

Strong hands smoothed her hair. Then, gently, trembling fingertips caressed her cheeks. Drewry had never seen a look more loving and tender than the one emanating from his dark eyes.

With one forefinger, he tilted her head and bent to touch her lips with his, feather-light at first, then longer and stronger until their breath mingled, and it seemed there was no air anywhere in the universe but the air they shared. This was nothing like the kiss she'd given him on the night of the fire. This kiss seemed to surge upward from the very depths of his soul, as if something long-buried in his heart was straining to break free.

She responded with her own soft sighs. "Chase," she murmured against his lips. "Oh, Chase . . ."

And then, just as easily, it seemed, as he'd captured her in the powerful circle of his embrace, Chase held her at arm's length and groaned. The mournful sound of it shattered the beautiful, magical moment their kiss had created. Pain glittered icily where warmth had glowed in his eyes. Without another word, he roughly shoved her aside and turned away, stomping off down the path.

For a moment only, she had allowed herself to believe that he might really care for her. *Silly girl,* she reminded herself, *unrequited love is as much as you can hope for with a man like Chase Auburn.* But for the rest of her life, she would remember the sensation of his lips against hers, the sound of his soft endearments in her ear, the feel of his strong hands pressing her close. Such a moment would never come again . . . not after the way he'd turned tail and run, like a rabbit with a hunter on its heels.

She stood alone on the path for a long time, unable to explain Chase's sudden departure. A squirrel, scampering in the branches overhead, roused her from her reverie. But even its comical antics and the shower of wild nuts it rained down upon her failed to produce a smile.

Woodenly, Drewry headed for the house, too stunned even to weep.

twelve

She hadn't slept a wink. The clock on her mantel told her it was nearly two in the morning.

Drewry paced her room, palms cupping elbows, as she gnawed at her lower lip. No matter how many times she replayed the tender scene in the woods, she couldn't understand why Chase had left her standing there alone.

She'd gone over every moment of their interlude time and again, asking herself if perhaps she'd offended him in some way. But no, each time the lovely picture presented itself in her memory, Drewry was forced to admit that nothing unpleasant had occurred. He had taken her in his arms as easily as he took breath, it seemed. His gentle voice caressed her ears with words of endearment. And his lips, surrounded by the thick handlebar mustache, had sought hers so sweetly.

She hadn't stiffened . . . nor had she behaved wantonly. Rather, she'd praised God for blessing her with proof that Chase felt about her as she did about him. The prayer was short, however, for even before Drewry had concluded, Chase had cut the kiss short.

He had seemed angry . . . no . . . *furious* more accurately described his mood when he made his abrupt departure. One moment, she was surrounded by two strong, loving arms; the next, she was standing alone on the path.

Drewry stopped her pacing and took a deep breath. When it failed to cleanse her mind and soul of the deep ache inside, she stepped out onto the balcony. There, in the muggy night air, she stared into the inky sky. The stars glittered from their velvety background. Drewry picked out the Big Dipper. Orion.

Sea captains set the course of their ships by looking into this same sky, Drewry knew. But what made them trust that those far-off sparkling diamonds would lead them safely from port to port, and home again? What did they see up there in the heavens that she didn't?

Suddenly, though she was surrounded by the vast sky above Magnolia Grange, Drewry felt closed in. Suffocated. Smothered.

Hurrying inside, she wrapped a plain black skirt around her white nightdress, then draped a fringed scarf around her shoulders. Her unbound hair flowed down her back like a nutmeg mane as she ran silently through the hall, down the grand staircase, across the foyer.

The moment her feet made contact with the rough, cool bricks of the front porch, she smiled, glad she hadn't bothered with boots. The soft coolness of the freshly mowed lawn felt comforting against her bare skin. She took her time getting from the front to the side yard, stopping now and then to wiggle her toes in the grass. The delicate scent of roses grew stronger as she neared the terrace.

Never in her months at Magnolia Grange had she been so bold as to pluck one, unless instructed to do so by Matilda. But the petals, glowing like silver velvet in the moonlight, invited her to cherish their beauty, and Drewry gave in to the temptation. The white blossom broke off more easily than she'd anticipated, and surprisingly, the thorns did her no harm.

She sat on the white iron bench that wrapped around the trunk of the maple tree nearest the terrace. Stroking the flower against her cheek, Drewry closed her eyes. Its silken petals reminded her of Chase's tender caress just before he'd lowered his head to hers that very afternoon. Her newly kissed lips now nuzzled the satiny bloom. *Why did you leave me like that?*

Drewry opened her eyes, surprised at the tears that blurred

her vision. Surely there were no more tears left . . .

Then something near the barn caught her attention. Something that glowed round and red, like the tip of a hot poker. She blinked, and it was gone. Drewry continued to stare at the spot for a moment longer, certain that all her exhaustive crying had caused a temporary lack of sanity.

But no . . . there it was again. And much closer this time!

She could smell it now, too. It was a cigar, like those that had clouded the air in Joshua Taylor's office, like the ones that fogged the dining room whenever Uncle James brought his gambling cronies home to play poker.

"You look mighty pretty sitting there in the moonlight," said a deep, rasping voice.

Drewry jumped to her feet and stifled a scream, cowering near the trunk of the tree.

"Take care with that rose now," he cautioned. "Pretty as they are, those thorns can leave a nasty scratch."

Finally, she found her voice. "Come out of the shadows and show yourself."

"Happy to oblige, pretty lady." The rotund figure of Sheriff Alden Kelly stepped into view.

Drewry wished now that she *had* screamed—screamed for all she was worth. "What are you doing here at this hour?" she demanded, hoping he wouldn't hear the fear trembling in her voice.

His grating laughter struck a deeper terror. "Why don't you tell me why *you* think I'm here . . ." He took several steps nearer, so close she could see her reflection in the black pinpoints of his pupils.

Though Drewry stood tall, the top of her head barely reached his shoulder. "You've no business here," she said firmly. "And if you don't leave at once, I'll call Mister Au—"

In seconds, Kelly was all around her, it seemed, as one hand snaked out and grabbed her wrist and the other clamped over her mouth. "You won't be callin' anybody, Miss High and Mighty." The sheriff started dragging her in the direction of the barn, scraping her bare feet and gashing her ankles on the flagstone path.

Drewry kicked. Pulled at his forearms. Pitched her body to and fro, and screamed against his sweaty, cigar-stinking palm.

"Now that's what I like," he said, chuckling under his breath. "A scrappy young thing that'll make it worth fightin' for."

A paralyzing fear nearly choked off her breath. Surely he didn't mean to . . .

When Kelly shoved her into the dark, hay-strewn barn, Drewry took a deep breath and opened her mouth to scream. "I wouldn't do that if I were you," he warned, his voice flowing sweet and slow as maple syrup in February.

She heard the unmistakable *click* of a pistol hammer locking into position, and pressed her trembling lips together.

"So she's smart as well as strong," Kelly said, nodding approvingly. "Good. Don't believe I've ever had me a smart woman before . . ."

"You won't get away with this," she said, backing away. "Someone will see or hear . . ." Now she was against the wall of the barn. There was nowhere else to go.

"I've been here often enough to know this place almost as well as I know my own. Nobody stirs 'round here at night. 'Specially after midnight." The man's evil snicker hung heavy on the humid air. "Guess you rich folks need all the beauty sleep you can get, eh?"

Drewry decided that no matter what happened, Sheriff Alden Kelly would know he'd been in a fight! She leaned against the rough wooden wall, watching . . . waiting . . .

Here now! What was that pressing into her spine?

Slipping her hand slowly behind her back, Drewry wrapped it around the handle of the pitchfork that hung on a peg just inside the door. If she were careful, very careful . . .

Kelly moved to the right. He hadn't lied. Obviously, he *had* been here often. How else would he have known precisely where the lantern hung? "Just a tad of light," he whispered, "for atmosphere."

She waited until he lifted the globe and struck the match before turning to seize her weapon. The leather strap by which it hung held it higher on the wall than she'd thought. Drewry tugged, lifted, tugged again, and still she wasn't able to get it down in one, fluid movement.

"Yes, indeedy," Kelly said, unhitching the pitchfork for her. "I do like 'em scrappy." He tossed the tool aside. It landed with a quiet *thump* on the floor of an empty stall.

Before she knew what was happening, Drewry was flat on her back on a bed of straw, looking up helplessly into the fat, leering face of Alden Kelly. The lantern cast a dim, eerie glow around the barn's interior, reminding Drewry of the haunted house the youth in her community had created one Halloween.

Kelly clamped a greasy palm over her mouth, then used one knee to pin her right arm to the floor, the other to keep her left arm in place. "Yes, indeedy," he said again, showing her his gap-toothed grin, "I do like 'em scrappy." Then, with his free hand, he grabbed the collar of her nightdress.

Chase! she screamed silently. *Chase, where are you!*

ꝫ

He'd been back and forth across the floor dozens of times, and considered it a minor miracle that his pacing hadn't worn a path in the Oriental carpeting. Chase stepped out onto his balcony and leaned his palms against the picket rail. *You've lost your mind, man,* he said to himself. *Whatever possessed you to kiss her that way?*

But he knew the answer to that question.

Drewry had inspired the kiss. And she'd done it simply by being herself. How wonderful she'd felt in his arms. How sweetly she'd melted against him, yielding to his tender kiss.

He'd thoroughly enjoyed the embrace, the soft whispering sounds of her sighs. But the image of Theresa suddenly entered his head, blotting out all rational thought. It didn't matter that she'd told him in plain language she *wanted* him to find another wife. It didn't matter that Claib and Matilda and Pastor Tillman had explained, time and again, that even God didn't expect him to remain alone, now that Theresa was gone.

But it was something Pastor Tillman had said at the cemetery that echoed round and round in his head: "You'll be reunited in Paradise. . . ." How could Chase rejoin Theresa in heaven after he'd been with another woman on earth?

Yes, he'd read it in the Bible for himself: Heaven was completely unlike earth. There would be no marriages there. Mark 12:25 explained it perfectly: "For when they shall rise from the dead, they neither marry, nor are given in marriage; but are as the angels which are in heaven." Still, Chase could not bring himself to begin a new romance. Not even with a woman as wonderful as Drewry Sheffield.

Matilda knew her charge well. She had placed an iron lawn chair on his balcony, with a matching white table beside it. Chase sat in the chair now and propped his feet on the table. Leaning back, he closed his eyes. A sense of unease, like none he'd ever felt before, settled over him. He opened his eyes and stared into the starry sky.

He could have sworn he heard Drewry's voice . . .

Yes . . . there it was again. And she was calling his name.

Chase sat up, straining to hear. A second passed, then two. Though he heard nothing, the sense that she needed him wrapped around his chest like an iron band, tightening as the seconds continued to tick silently by.

Standing, Chase peered across the dew-dampened yard. He continued to glance to and fro, until his gaze rested upon the barn, some hundred yards in the distance. *Is that a light in the window?* he wondered, squinting. *Yes, it it is a light.*

The very idea alarmed Chase. After witnessing firsthand the quick destructiveness of fire, he had no desire to see the scene repeated. He dashed down the stairs, not even bothering to close the front door behind him, and ran toward the dim glow.

He had but a dozen yards to go when he heard scuffling sounds. Claib had moved the horses to an outbuilding near the servant's cottages, so that he could repair the roof, damaged in the last thunderstorm. Since no animals boarded there, the noises confused Chase. Perhaps a cat, or a family of field mice . . .

Chase stopped dead in his tracks and keened his ear toward the barn doors. *That's a man's voice!* Though Chase couldn't make out what the fellow was saying, the throaty, guttural laughter made it patently clear that he was up to no good.

That's when he heard for the first time the soft, muffled cries of a woman. *Drewry!*

Everything in him told him to barge in and lift the man by his hair, then beat the living daylights out of him. If he'd harmed her in any way . . . But Chase knew better than to rush in without a plan. Whoever held her there against her will would no doubt react in violence if he felt threatened.

Chase must plan his strategy well. But he had to work quickly.

Sneaking around to the back side of the barn, he peered through the filmy window. There, on his hands and knees, was Alden Kelly and beneath him, Drewry cried and thrashed about for dear life.

Chase would go in through the side door. Claib had constructed a wooden hallway of sorts just inside, to keep the cattle immobile during branding. An assortment of iron tools would be within easy reach. Chase stepped softly to avoid making a sound that might warn Kelly of his approach.

Slowly, he slipped in through the narrow opening. Just as

he expected, iron bars and rods hung by leather thongs on the barn wall. Chase eased one from its wooden peg, biting his lip, as if doing so would assure his silence.

Then he made his move.

"Turn her loose, Kelly!"

Kelly, red-faced and sweating, turned toward the sound of Chase's voice. "Well," he said to Drewry, "what have we here? Your boss-man has warm feelin's for you, does he?"

"He's got a gun, Chase!" she warned, her words muffled by the pressure of Kelly's palm. "Go away. Please! Run!"

She could see that Chase hadn't understood. Drewry tried again to sink her teeth into Kelly's palm. But his evil laughter told her she hadn't succeeded. So she did the only thing left to do, and with her eyes implored Chase to leave the barn. "Before you get hurt," she muttered. "The children . . . Don't let him make orphans of them!"

Chase lunged forward. Somehow, miraculously, he stood behind Kelly, gripping the branding iron with both hands . . . against the lout's throat!

Kelly sputtered and choked, but he never let go of Drewry. Grabbing a handful of her hair, he pulled her with him as Chase lifted him off his feet. "I'll blow her head clean off, Auburn," Kelly gasped. "Le'go of me, or I'll shoot her right before your very eyes!"

Chase's gaze sought Drewry's. *I'll do whatever he asks to save you,* he seemed to be saying.

In that instant, Kelly managed to wriggle free of Chase's hold, dropping his pistol in the process. But he still had Drewry by the hair—his ticket to freedom. "I've gotcha right where I want ya," he sneered. As added insurance, he lifted the lighted lantern and held it high in his free hand. "I'll make ya a deal, Auburn."

Chase only glared at him.

"Give me the girl, and I won't burn down your barn."

Chase frowned. "Do whatever you want, Kelly," he bit out. "Nothing I own is as important as Drewry."

Kelly removed a stick of dynamite from the back pocket of his trousers, then shoved Drewry forward and into Chase's arms. She clung to him with one hand, trembling and sobbing as she tried to hold the bodice of her gown closed with the other.

"Gotta have somethin' to tell the boys about my visit here tonight," he said by way of explanation. "You have 'til the count of ten," Kelly said, stooping to retrieve his pistol, "before I blow this drafty old barn of yours to smithereens."

Chase guided Drewry toward the door. "You'll pay for this, Kelly."

"No, I won't. And we both know it." Kelly tossed his head back and cut loose with a stream of maniacal laughter. In a moment, he composed himself. "One, two, three . . ." he began, using the pistol as a pointer. "I'd get on outta here if I was you . . ."

Chase and Drewry stepped through the door.

"Four, five, six . . ."

"Run, Drewry, run!" Chase hollered, grabbing her hand. Only then did he notice that she was limping on bloodied, bruised feet. He didn't waste a moment, but scooped her up in his arms and ran with her toward the house.

"Seven, eight, nine!" Kelly shouted after them. "I'm lightin' the match . . . I'm holding it to the fuse . . ."

Something must have gone terribly wrong, Chase knew. That fuse had been no less than two feet long, yet suddenly, Kelly's grating laughter was drowned out by the dynamite's detonation. Boards and nails flew in all directions. Chase, fearing a shard might gore Drewry, pushed her to the ground and threw himself on top of her.

A blood-curdling bellow punctuated the explosion. Chase lifted his head in time to see Sheriff Alden Kelly, staggering around the barnyard, clutching his barrel chest. The force of the blast had driven a large sword-shaped splinter of wood directly through his heart.

He was dead before he hit the ground.

❧

Drewry held the mug in both trembling hands as she sat huddled under the quilt Matilda had draped around her shoulders. "I'm fine," she insisted through swollen, bruised lips. "Really. All this fuss and bother is unnecessary."

"Nonsense, girl," the big woman said. "You is gonna drink that milk, then you is gonna climb into bed and get some shut-eye."

She hadn't been able to argue when Matilda insisted on drawing her a hot bath. Drewry didn't imagine she'd be able to argue this point, either. She smiled feebly. "Thank you. Thank you all."

"No thanks nec'sary," Claib said. "You is family, Miss Drew, an' we take good care of our own."

Chase hadn't said much since she'd hobbled into the kitchen. It had been a stupid, foolish thing to go outside alone in the dark. She knew that now. "But goin' outdoors with no shoes on," Matilda scolded, hands propped on her beefy hips, "in the dead o' night when you can't see where you is goin' . . . ." The woman could only shake her head. "What was you thinkin', Miss Drewry?"

Drewry stared at her reflection on the surface of the milk. "I don't know," she lied.

She knew exactly what she'd been thinking. She'd been trying to understand why Chase had so callously left her there on the path through the woods after their passionate embrace.

In the tub earlier, she'd thought of that moment, too. But not nearly so often as she'd thought of the way he'd sacrificed his barn—and all the tools in it—for her! He'd sacrificed his property for her, whereas her own uncle had sacrificed *her* for property. She trembled visibly at the memory of Alden Kelly, gripping the bloody stake that had ended his life.

Chase, seeing her trembling, was beside her in an instant. Gently, he used a dampened towel to dab at the cuts on her lips. "Did he . . . did he hurt you?" he asked, his voice quavering slightly.

"No," she said truthfully. "No, he didn't . . . thanks to you."

With a grateful sigh, Chase pressed the cool cloth to her forehead.

"I'm fine. Really," she insisted, waving him away.

But he refused to obey. "We almost lost you tonight, Drewry. I'm so very grateful the Good Lord heard my prayers . . ."

She looked at him then. At the soulful brown eyes and the worried brow. At the tense set of his powerful jaw. "You . . . you *prayed* for me?"

Chase snorted. "Why wouldn't I? You mean so very much to—to all of us here at Magnolia Grange."

Had he hesitated because he'd wanted to say she meant something to *him?* Her heart soared at the mere possibility.

"It's time you get on up to bed, Miss Drew," Matilda ordered. "Mistah Chase, you want Claib an' Simon to carry her, so's she don't have to walk on them poor feet?"

Chase shook his head. "No. I'll take her up."

Matilda didn't seem at all surprised by his answer. With a huff and a puff, she put Drewry's mug into the sink. "Y'all get on outta here now," she said to Claib and Simon. "The rooster be crowin' mighty early in the mornin', an' I ain't gonna ring the breakfast bell more'n once!"

Ignoring Matilda's flapdoodle, Chase gently slipped one arm behind Drewry's knees, the other behind her back, and lifted her from the chair. "You'll tell me if I hurt you . . ."

She wrapped her arms around his neck. "You couldn't hurt me, Chase Auburn," she said—not with an air of arrogance, but with an inner certainty. "You couldn't hurt *anyone*."

"I could have killed Kelly tonight," he said, climbing the stairs slowly and carefully as he cradled her in his arms like a rare treasure.

Drewry shook her head. "You'd have hurt him, maybe. But you'd never have killed him. At least, not on purpose."

"And how is it you know so much, Drewry Sheffield?"

Their lips were only inches apart. Drewry could have kissed him, if only she leaned forward just a bit. But she didn't dare. Not after the way he'd behaved that afternoon. *Oh, but I don't know you, Chase Auburn,* she thought, swallowing a sob. *And I doubt I ever shall.*

ⁱ

Long after he'd gently closed her bedchamber door, Drewry lay awake, her mind whirling. She was sure Chase didn't love her . . . at least, not the way a man loves a woman; Matilda and Claib were dead wrong about that! But he did care about her. That much was evident in the cautious way he'd tended her injuries, in the easy way he'd carried her upstairs, in the sweetness of his smile as he blew out the light.

She took a deep breath and stretched out under the covers. *Some folks live a lifetime without experiencing one true-blue friendship,* she told herself as she closed her eyes. *If nothing else, Chase is your friend. Be thankful for that much.*

It wouldn't keep her from wishing their relationship could be more. But she'd promised Matilda that she was going to begin behaving like a grown-up. And she would begin tomorrow. No more hang-dog expressions. No more late-night pouting sessions. No more wishing upon stars for what could never be.

Drewry wasn't *happy* about the fact that Chase would never be more than a good and loving friend, but the fact didn't distress her, either. He had very likely saved her life tonight.

Thank You, God, she prayed, *for letting Chase hear my plea tonight. Thank You for sending him to save me from that awful man. And be merciful to Alden Kelly . . .*

Chase's behavior was proof that he was her friend. The thought lulled her, and for the first time in days, Drewry slept— the deep, contented slumber of a child.

thirteen

Chase paced back and forth, his booted footsteps echoing on the hardwood floor. At this late hour, his library provided welcome solitude. The only light came from the moon, burnishing the room with its ethereal whiteness. He needed privacy to mull over the night's strange events and to seek divine guidance for his confused feelings.

Memories lingered to haunt him. The hurt that had ripped across Drewry's countenance when he had pushed her away this afternoon. Her anguish and terror when he'd burst into the barn and interrupted Alden Kelly's shameful business. Drewry's pleading cries that, even now, tore at his heart. The stench of dynamite. The heat of the blazing barn . . .

As a Christian and a gentleman, what choice had he? A barn could be replaced. Drewry's honor could not. At least, he'd been in time to spare that, despite the heartache he'd caused her earlier that day.

Chase stopped pacing and ran his hand through his thick, dark hair, his thoughts churning. He took a deep breath and looked out the window toward the shadow of the trees, where Kelly had met his end. For a man who usually knew his own feelings as well as he knew his children, Chase had to admit he was stumped. He hadn't planned on kissing Drewry, but at the time, the action seemed so right. So natural. Until, in the middle of it, he had remembered Theresa . . .

But it was the violence of his emotions in the barn that had shaken him to the core.

The great wellspring of fury he'd felt for Drewry's assailant, the urge to protect her—an urge which would have driven him to throw himself into Kelly's line of fire if necessary—went far beyond the duty of employer to employee. This much he knew.

Emotions of such magnitude rightly belonged to a husband, whose holy vow it was to protect and honor his beloved wife, even at the cost of his own life. But the instant he'd realized the danger Drewry was in, this jealous anger had risen involuntarily from the depths of his being. Nobody would hurt her, not while there was breath in his body!

Chase sank into the big brown chair beside the fireplace and buried his face in his hands. He was not Drewry's husband. He was *Theresa's* husband.

Painfully, he lifted his head and forced himself to focus on the empty chair opposite his. Theresa's chair. Since her arrival at Magnolia Grange, however, it had been Drewry's choice of seating. Now it was rightfully hers. She had earned that place. Night after night, she'd sat there, keeping him company, sharing the rearing of his children, sharing the most private thoughts of his mind—and sometimes the secrets of his heart.

Ah, yes. *Secrets.*

Miss Drewry Sheffield was definitely guarding some secret. Chase knew it. He could feel it, deep in his bones. She either wouldn't—or couldn't—share the whole truth about herself and her past with him. Her secrecy hurt him so deeply that Chase started in surprise. Slowly, it dawned on him that his pain at her lack of trust came because he wanted so badly to share her life—the good and the bad—as completely as only a . . . *husband* . . . could.

Chase sprang to his feet, strode over to the hearth, and leaned his head wearily against the massive, carved mantelpiece. Retrieving Theresa's picture from his pocket, he studied it. How could he be a husband to Drewry while he was still married to Theresa? He turned the ferrotype over and read the message Theresa had inscribed there: "Until death do us part."

Strange that he hadn't thought of that particular part of his marriage vows since the moment he'd spoken them. Death had seemed so remote on their wedding day, a day filled with the promise of life. Now he wondered why Theresa had chosen that phrase above all the others. Suddenly, he had the sensation that she was reaching back to him, gently untying the knot that bound him to her.

Until death do us part. Tears streamed down his face as he stared at the words until they blurred. Death had parted them. It had been God's will; it was Chase who had refused to let go.

He closed his eyes and held the picture against his heart. "Thank you, Theresa, for the love we shared and for the beautiful children you gave me," he said softly. "You have preceded me to the next life, my darling. Please understand and forgive me if I follow your suggestion and allow the bonds of love to grow between myself and Drewry. I will cherish you no less."

Chase sighed heavily, feeling a weight lift from his heart. He remembered Theresa's last wifely admonition—to find a new love—and he smiled. How well she had known him. How well she had loved him.

Reverently, he kissed her likeness and set the picture on the mantelpiece, propped against a vase of marigolds and irises that Sally had arranged for him that morning. He admired the smiling face and felt that Theresa was bestowing her blessing.

He threw himself into his chair and for a long time, gazed at the cold gray ashes in the grate. Drewry was safely asleep in her bed, drugged slightly by one of Matilda's herbal teas. Before he revealed the depth of his feelings to her, he must wait until she trusted him enough to share her secret. Yes, he'd wait—as patiently and expectantly as he waited for the seedlings to break through the fertile soil into the sunlight. He'd wait, because love had to be grounded in trust.

Besides—and he chuckled softly in anticipation—how bad

could his Lady Nanny's secret be?

ૹ

> *Freetown, Maryland*
> *August 16, 1868*

> *Dear Miss Drewry,*
>   *May the Lord be praised!*
>   *Ain't nothing too hard for our God to accomplish. His deeds are truly wondrous to behold. I is talking about your uncle. Just like the prodigal son, he done come back to the Lord.*
>   *It has lots to do with Miss Naomi and her preacher daddy, but Mister James ain't coming back just to please his lady friend. No siree. He come back to the Lord in his heart. He be a changed man, Miss Drew, a new creature in Christ.*
>   *Yesterday, he tell me the truth about who I is. I always suspected, but I never knowed for sure. Me and Mister James, we have the same daddy, Abraham Sheffield! Mister James showed me proof—papers that ole Abe left behind. It explains why you say so many times that I look like Abe when I smile. Me and Mister James is half-brothers! He say he ain't ashamed to be related to a black. He say we is all God's children. Well, if me and Mister James is kin, you and me is kin, too! I couldn't love you more, kin or no kin. But I think you already knowed that.*
>   *Truth is a powerful healing thing. It sets the soul free. Give your Mister Chase a chance to prove that he be a good Christian. Tell him the truth, and set yourself free.*

> *Forgive this ole man for rambling and*
> *preaching so, but you is my niece, girl, and I*
> *only wants what is best for you.*
>
> > *Your affectionate uncle,*
> > *Jeb Sheffield*

> *P.S. Mister James be planning to travel to*
> *Richmond to meet you and patch things up. I*
> *know he cause you a passel of grief, but remem-*
> *ber, we is to forgive others as we has been*
> *forgive.*

ॐ

Drewry reread Jeb's letter four times during the carriage ride into Richmond. Things had been happening so quickly, her mind was a blur. The letter had arrived only hours before James's telegraph, inviting her to afternoon tea at the Chesterfield Hill Hotel.

Her grip on the letter tightened. Tears welled in her eyes. She'd gained two uncles, all in one day! Dear Jeb! Why, she'd loved him like an uncle, even before the proof was uncovered. And James . . . changed? Could she dare believe that God had given her back her old Uncle James, the one she could trust and depend upon?

She tucked the letter into her purse and checked her list. Not wanting to tell Chase that she was meeting Uncle James, she'd drawn up a shopping list as an excuse to go into town. Not that Chase would mind her meeting her uncle—of that she had no doubt—but she wasn't yet ready to tell him about her past.

As she swept into the grand lobby of the Chesterfield, with its imposing marble staircase, thick red carpets, enormous chandeliers and stately, high ceilings, Drewry absorbed the elegance that seemed to permeate every inch of the hotel. The owner ushered her into the private parlor where, he informed her,

Mr. James Sheffield awaited her.

Leaning on his cane, James stood the moment she appeared in the doorway. Drewry gasped and blinked back the tears that suddenly flooded her eyes. A clean, handsome, sober man with a neatly trimmed black beard stood before her. A man whose clear blue eyes twinkled with the warmth and good humor she remembered so well from childhood. A man who respectfully waited for her gesture of greeting . . . and forgiveness.

"Uncle James!" Ignoring all ladylike reserve, she threw down her purse and flew to him.

"My precious Drew-girl," he said, opening his arms as she flung herself against him. "Thank the Lord! I was afraid you wouldn't show up. I certainly don't deserve it after the way I treated you."

Drewry pulled back, just a little, to look up into his eyes and to touch his soft, dark beard. "Oh, Uncle," she sighed. "How could I *not* forgive you? I *love* you!"

Tears shimmered in his sky-blue eyes. "Thank you, honey," he said softly, shaking his head. "God knows I don't deserve that love, but by His grace, I'll never do you wrong again. And that's a promise."

Drewry gazed helplessly at him, dazed by happiness, until they were interrupted by an elderly waiter in a long black morning coat. "Tea is served," he announced stiffly.

Offering his arm to Drewry, James gave a little nod. "Shall we? A toast to forgiveness—with nothing stronger than tea and cream, of course."

He led her to the small, round table in front of the window of their private room. The delicacy of the lace tablecloth, the gleam of the silver, the white translucence of the china—none of this beauty could add one whit to the joy in Drewry's heart. Her cup was overflowing already!

"I have so much to explain," James said as he passed her the silver tray, lined with cucumber sandwiches.

"You needn't . . ." she began.

James held up a hand to silence her. "But I must, Drew-girl. As part of my new life in Christ, I want to make things right with you—to confess my . . . deception."

Her eyes grew round. "Deception?"

James steepled his hands, took a deep breath, and focused on Drewry's face. "This is not an easy thing to admit . . . but I'm not the war hero everyone thinks I am."

Drewry found herself fiddling nervously with the embroidered trim along the edge of her napkin. "Oh?"

"I deserve a medal all right—for ingenuity in cowardice." He took a deep, shuddering breath. "My last battle, all my men were dying around me. After the shot to my head, I'd fallen and, like the coward I was, I stayed down and played dead."

Drewry studied her uncle's face. She saw pain there, but not the kind of crazed pain she'd witnessed during his drunken ramblings. This pain was different—serene, hopeful. Pain that had known forgiveness.

James cleared his throat and continued. "I was wounded, as you know." Unconsciously, his hand strayed to the jagged scar on his face. "But this foot wound . . . well, that wasn't the result of a Yankee bullet."

Drewry blinked. "It wasn't?"

"No." He dropped his gaze, unable to meet her eyes. "I'm afraid I'll have to take credit for that one. . . . I took out my pistol and shot myself in the foot so there'd be no questions asked."

Without a moment's hesitation, Drewry reached across the table and placed her hand on his. "Uncle James . . ." Her heart went out to him. How he must have suffered all these years.

"That's not the worst of it," he admitted sadly. "After I did it, one of my men, dying beside me, struggled to turn his head toward me. He managed to choke out only three words . . . no more. But those three words have echoed in my mind all these years—haunting, accusing . . ."

Drewry nodded encouragingly, still clinging to his hand. "Yes. Go on. What did he say?"

"It's not what he said—it's what he asked me . . ." James's voice trailed off, and he took a deep breath before continuing his painful story. "His last words were, 'How could you?'" Suddenly, James looked older than his years. "So maybe you can see now, Drewry, why I tried to escape into the bottle. I'm not excusing my behavior, mind you . . . but it's important to me that you understand why I did the things I did. I couldn't live with my conscience. I couldn't live with the *lie* . . ."

It was Drewry's turn to drop her head as Uncle James talked on, venting the years of guilt and frustration.

"Looking back at the irresponsible young man I was before the Confederacy made an officer of me, I can see how the burden of leadership was too much for me. But the cowardly ways I chose to deal with that immaturity . . . well, now I know that my actions are my responsibility alone. I have no one to blame but myself."

Drewry's eyes sparkled with unshed tears. She understood so much now . . . about her uncle . . . about herself. "Uncle James," was all she could manage.

"God is merciful," he said, brightening a bit. "He sent a messenger of mercy in the form of Naomi, my beautiful Indian princess. She brought me the love and forgiveness of God." James smiled, his eyes filling with light. "But that's another story. Today, I only wanted to tell you the ugly truth about myself and beg your forgiveness. Will you, Drew-girl? *Can* you forgive me?"

She swallowed hard. The nibbles she'd taken of her cucumber sandwich felt like boulders in her throat. "I'm so sorry for

the pain you've lived with. I'll agree that you may have brought
some of it on yourself, but it doesn't change the fact that you've
suffered tremendously. Of course, I forgive you, Uncle." She
smiled a watery smile. "And I'm happy that you told me the
truth. That took great courage . . ." *More courage than* I
have, Drewry admitted to herself.

James squeezed her hand gratefully. "Oh, Drew-girl, waiting to see how you'd take the news was far more painful than
telling it. My worst fear was that I'd lost my little niece forever. Especially after that Porter Hopkins stunt." He looked
away, shaking his head sadly. "I still can't believe I could
have done such a vile and despicable thing."

"Neither can I."

At that he glanced up, surprised to see her expression. "It
was a shameful thing to do . . . to take a beautiful, intelligent
girl like you and . . ." He broke off with a sigh. "Well, you
deserve the best man God ever created, not some oaf like
Hopkins." James chuckled in spite of himself. "You should
have seen him when I told him you'd run off. His face turned
as red as a pot of stewed beet roots. I thought he'd die of a
stroke right there and then!"

Drewry giggled. "I wish I could have been around to see
that!" After a short pause, she added, "It all seems so silly
now . . . But however did you get back the deed to Plumtree
Orchards?"

"Old Jeb to the rescue, of course. He called the minister,
who called the judge, and we worked things out. Wasn't legal
for me to gamble you away in the first place. Oh, Drewry," he
moaned, "I was out of my mind! What can I do to make it up
to you?"

She shook her head. "Having you back in my life—the way
you were before—is an answer to prayer."

James winked. "Well, if it's any consolation, I promise never
to gamble you away again. But I'd gladly *give* you away . . . to

the bridegroom of your choice! Now, what's this I hear about a handsome employer?"

Drewry shifted nervously on the tufted, velvet-cushioned chair. "He's handsome, all right. And brave enough to stand up to a gang of Klansmen, yet gentle enough to be a loving father." She averted her gaze, and focused on the candelabra on the fireplace mantel across the room. "But I don't know that he cares for me . . . romantically, that is."

"Drew-girl, any man who'd pass you up has got to be as crazy as I was on the night I gambled you away."

Drewry met his loving gaze and smiled sadly. "Tell me about Jeb," she said, trying to steer the conversation away from Chase and his obvious lack of interest in her. "How did he react when he discovered that Grandfather was his daddy?"

"His feet haven't touched the ground since I told him we're half-brothers," James said, smiling.

"You knew all this time, and didn't tell him?"

His face flushed dark red beneath the black beard. "Yes, though I'm ashamed to admit it."

"But, Uncle, you always told me the truth when I was a child. Don't you remember when Muffin died? You were the only one who was honest with me. And what about when Mama and Papa were killed? Only *you* would tell me what really happened."

"Yes, yes, I remember," he said hastily. "But you see, Drewry, I told you the truth, because it was an *easy* truth. It's easy to tell a little girl that her puppy died. But it's harder to come clean about family secrets and personal inadequacy. Jeb . . . my assigning officer." He cleared his throat. "I should have told Jeb the truth about his parentage, should have admitted to my assigning officer that I hadn't the experience to lead men in battle. But, in both cases, pride was standing in the way. I'm afraid I went for cheap honesty . . ."

"'Cheap honesty?'" Drewry echoed in surprise.

"Honesty that didn't cost me much." James cracked a grin that reached all the way to his clear blue eyes. "Yeah, cheap honesty can make a fellow feel downright self-righteous. Hardly the kind of honesty Christ was talking about."

Cheap honesty. The concept stirred something deep within Drewry. It was easy to be honest with Sally and Sam. They were only children, after all, and they gave their trust so freely. But to be honest with Chase when she could risk losing him— losing almost everything and everyone she had come to love— well, that was honesty of a more expensive variety, to be sure.

"Uncle James," she began, leaning forward earnestly, "I'd like to ask your advice about a situation I find myself in—a situation where cheap honesty just isn't good enough . . ."

fourteen

Autumn came early to Richmond that year, bringing with it chilly evenings and brisk mornings. Drewry was forced to begin giving Sally and Sam their lessons inside, much to their dismay.

On one particularly cool October morning, however, Drewry suggested they take their "classroom" outside once again, where they could pick up leaf samples from those that blanketed the lawn. There, sitting on a thick patchwork quilt Drewry had spread on the ground, they discussed plant structure and construction. She taught the children that pigments, developing in the cells of the leaves, and decomposition of chlorophyll, caused the red and yellow and orange colors, and that every leaf leaves a scar when it falls from the tree.

Sally was amazed by the phenomenon. "But, Drewry," she said, looking up at the still-leafy branches overhead, "there are millions and millions of leaves on those trees . . ."

Drewry nodded her agreement.

"Oh!" the child exclaimed. "The poor trees! That means they'll have millions and millions of scars!"

Sam seemed disturbed by the information and reminded Drewry how he'd fallen out of his red wagon the week before, scraping both knees on the flagstone walk that bordered the house. "Doo-ree," he said, placing his tiny hand in hers, "when the leafs fall off, does it hurt the trees?"

Drewry smiled and gently stroked his cheek. "No, Sam. Not a bit."

Tentatively, he touched each brown scab. "I started to peel one," he began, wincing at the memory, "but it hurted. Matilda said if I tooked it off, it would leave a scar." He stood up again. "If it hurted me to get a scar, why wouldn't it hurt the trees?"

"Because, when God created the trees," Drewry explained, "He made sure they'd feel no pain."

She thought about the science lesson long after the children had gone inside to take their afternoon naps. *Millions of leaves—millions of scars,* she recalled, yet the trees feel no pain at all. *If only human hearts could be as sturdy!* Drewry sighed, recalling the way Chase had rejected her that day on the woodland path.

But enough self-pity! Drewry scolded herself. She'd made a promise to Matilda—and to herself—to stop whimpering about things that could never be and to start behaving like an adult. With a determined spring in her step, she retrieved her latest book from her desk and brought it out to the terrace. There, beneath a fuzzy woolen coverlet, she read *Water Babies* and sipped warm apple cider from one of the big white mugs that hung on the wall above Matilda's spanking clean stove.

She'd been sitting there in the sunshine for less than half an hour when the wind picked up. Crisp brown leaves skittered across the stone terrace floor, making soft scratching noises. The blanket she'd draped across her knees refused to stay tucked, and the pages of Charles Kingsley's wonderfully whimsical tale fluttered like bird wings.

Drewry looked beyond the hip-high stone wall that surrounded the terrace, shocked at the sudden bleakness of the fall sky. Quickly she moved to gather her things and go inside, where it was warm.

For the remainder of the afternoon, the wind whistled menacingly through the pines, bending the trunks of fragile willows and birch in the woods beyond the lawn. Pinecones rolled hither and yon, making Drewry think of the stories she'd read of the nation's wild, wild West, where tumbleweeds bounced across the landscape like huge round cages. The small woodland creatures that generally scampered at the edge of the forest at this time of day, foraging for food, were nowhere to be seen.

And all through Matilda's delicious dinner of roasted chicken and baby potatoes, butter beans and beets, and popovers—Chase's boyhood favorite—the wind soughed through the eaves of the manor house. Bridget had just passed through the swinging door that separated the kitchen from the dining room when a great blast of air blew a pane from one of the windows. The chilly gust doused all six candles in the chandelier, casting the dining room into near darkness.

"Stay calm, everyone," Chase ordered, with a quiet air of authority. "No need to panic."

Sam and Sally huddled with Bridget at the far end of the massive table as the tablecloth lifted like a giant white sail, overturning water goblets and serving bowls. Silverware clattered against the rose-patterned china. Milk, tea, and cider dripped onto the hardwood floor with a steady *plop, plop, plop.* Matilda and Drewry gathered up the linen napkins and began to mop up the spills.

Chase darted from the room, and returned moments later with hammer, nails, and a piece of wood slightly larger than the missing pane of glass. "Drewry," he called over his shoulder, "would you come here and hold this for me while I fasten it in place?"

She hurried to oblige, not realizing how unnerving his nearness would be. Her heart beat erratically as she inhaled the pleasant masculine scent of him as he stooped over to reach the bottom windowpane.

He had removed his black dinner jacket and tie and rolled up the sleeves of his starched white shirt, exposing the muscles of his forearms. He worked quickly but efficiently, taking care not to damage the carved wood trim as he nailed the board over the offending hole.

"There. I believe that ought to do it," he announced, straightening to his full height.

It never ceased to amaze Drewry how it pleased Chase to work with his hands. His powerful, sinewy hands . . .

"You younguns go on up to your rooms now and play for a spell," Matilda instructed. "Soon as Bridget an' me get this mess cleared up, we'll serve dessert." With that, the two women disappeared into the kitchen.

The children cowered near the door, obviously too frightened to climb the stairs alone—not as long as the mournful wailing of the wind continued outside.

"Chase," Drewry whispered near his ear, "would it be all right if the children joined me in the parlor instead? We could play backgammon or checkers until the storm passes."

Chase studied the worried faces of his son and daughter. "A splendid idea," he agreed in a conspiratorial whisper. "I'll join you there shortly." Then, to the children he said, "Perhaps if you ask her very politely, Drewry will play you a tune on the harpsichord."

Immediately, their faces brightened and they skipped off to wait in the parlor for the adults.

"I don't recall telling you that I could play the harpsichord."

He grinned wickedly. "Didn't have to tell me. I've heard you playing when you thought no one was about." With a wave of the hammer he was returning to Claib, he disappeared into the kitchen.

❧

Drewry played until her fingers cramped and sang until her voice was hoarse, choosing lively tunes that would, she hoped, drown out the dreadful groaning of the wind. When the time came to tuck the children in for the night, she promised to leave their bedchamber doors ajar, so the dim light of the hall lanterns would filter into their rooms.

Drewry understood their fears, for she'd experienced a restless agitation herself all evening, thanks to the ceaseless wind. Shortly after the children drifted off to sleep, the sky opened up and pelted the earth with sheets of icy rain and hailstones.

Chase had retired to his library when she led the children upstairs for bed. Now, as she sat beside the fire in the downstairs parlor, she could hear his booted footsteps thudding back and forth across the carpeted floor. *If even Chase, who's always so controlled and calm, is on edge, it must mean that Mother Nature is brewing up something horrible.*

Sipping the tea Bridget had delivered only moments ago, Drewry shivered. She simply *had* to calm down. What sort of nanny was she if she couldn't remain composed on behalf of her young charges?

Hoping to lose herself in the pages of a book, she took up where she had left off that afternoon. Then, coming to the conclusion of *Water Babies,* she rose to make another selection—Charles Dickens's *Great Expectations*—from a stack of books on the table. She had expected to be mesmerized, as always, by the words of the popular author. Instead, lulled by the constant sighing of the wind, she snuggled deeper beneath the crocheted afghan on the divan and drifted off to sleep.

❧

He hadn't meant to stand there gawking like a love-struck schoolboy, but then, he hadn't expected to find her curled up on the parlor couch like a contented kitten, either. She was a vision, lying there, Chase thought, her long lashes curving gently up from her rosy cheeks, her dark curls splayed out across the cushions like a chestnut fan. Draped in the afghan, she looked like the Italian painting of a guardian angel he'd seen displayed at the art museum on his last trip to New York.

Chase might have stood there, staring, until she woke, had a clap of thunder not startled him nearly out of his boots. He ran to the parlor window and parted the red velvet draperies. The storm showed no signs of abating any time soon.

His soy crop experiments! The plants could never withstand such a storm! And what of the delicate panes of glass in the hothouse? With this new dilemma creasing his brow, Chase thundered toward the foyer and grabbed his rain slicker from the hall tree, then dashed outside, slamming the heavy door behind him.

Drewry woke with a start, wondering whether the noise she'd heard had been thunder or the slamming of a door. She bolted upright on the sofa, her heart pounding in her chest. Something told her that this time she knew the source of the crashing sound.

She stood alone in the hall for a moment, craning her ear to hear if Chase was still pacing in his library.

Silence.

Drewry tiptoed down the hall to peek into his private chamber.

Empty.

Perhaps he'd gone into the kitchen for a sip of water or a slice of pie.

No one was about.

The grandfather clock in the hall said nine forty-five . . . too early for Chase to retire, especially on a night like this.

And then, as surely as if an angel had whispered his whereabouts in her ear, Drewry knew where she would find him.

Grabbing her slicker from the hall tree, she ran outside, securing the door behind her. He was in that field, no doubt, hovering over that ever-loving experiment of his. *What can he be thinking!* she ranted to herself, holding the hood of her raincoat over her head. *He could be struck by lightning, or felled by a tree branch, or . . .* Drewry didn't want to consider the possibilities.

And what are you *thinking, Drewry Sheffield,* she chided herself, *running after him this way?* The chances of finding him were slim, at best, what with the pounding rain and unrelenting wind. Why, in all likelihood, *he'd* have to send a search party out to rescue *her* before it was all over! But she pushed on, peering through the darkness.

A bolt of lightning sliced the black sky, and she saw him then, silhouetted by the silvery glare. She opened her mouth to call out his name, but a harsh clap of thunder drowned her out.

She'd have to go to him. He'd chastise her, no doubt, but he'd chastised her before. She was becoming accustomed to his scoldings.

It seemed like hours instead of minutes before she reached him, coming up behind him. He stood there, looking every bit as forlorn as he had on the night the Klan had set fire to the other field. Following the direction of his gaze, she understood his anguish. This field, too, had been destroyed.

"Chase," she called, moving to stand alongside him, "come back to the house. I'll fix us a mug of warm milk . . ."

Slowly, he turned to face her. "What are you doing out here?" he shouted above the din of the storm, the rain—or was it tears?—wet on his cheeks. His voice was filled with the sound of his torment. "Why do you insist upon witnessing all my weakest moments!"

She shook her head. "I—I was . . . worried about you," she stammered. As with Uncle James, self-pity was an ugly thing. She'd come to expect more—better—from Chase. It unnerved her to see him behaving like a normal, flesh-and-blood man. How dare he stand there, assuming a defeated posture, sounding like a lost little boy! "I came," she added, her voice firm and strong now, "because I care about you, Chase Auburn!"

Chase took her in his arms and held her tight, then led her to a nearby shed that offered protection from the driving rain. "I'm sorry, Drewry," he breathed against her hair, "so sorry to have shouted at you that way."

Drewry returned his hug. "It's all right, Chase," she soothed, comforting him as she would have one of the children. "It'll be all right. You'll see . . ."

She felt, rather than heard, his heaving sigh. "I'm so grateful for you, Drewry. No matter how badly I've behaved or how cruelly I've spoken to you, you've been steadfast . . . a loyal friend."

He pushed back the hood of her raincoat, then gently cupped

her face in his hands. "I'm a very fortunate man to have a friend I can share my troubles with—without fear of judgment or scorn."

Then, softly, so softly that she scarcely felt the pressure of his lips, Chase dropped a kiss on her forehead. "Yes, I'm a lucky man . . . and that's the truth."

Truth. . . . truth . . . truth. The word echoed in her head, spinning and tumbling and leaving her stunned and breathless. This was the moment she had been dreading, the inevitable moment. It was time to tell Chase the truth.

"Let's go back now," she said, holding out her hand.

He took one last sad look at his ravaged field. Nodding, he put his hand into hers. "Yes, it's time," he agreed. "There's nothing we can do here. It's lost. But praise the Lord, everyone who means anything to me is safe."

On the way back to the house, she strained to make him hear her. Maybe it would be easier if she could say what she had to say out here. "There is something I must tell you, Chase."

"Another confession?" he called back with a grin.

Her heart thundered, louder it seemed, than the storm raging about them. "I'm not the person you think I am!"

He raised one dark brow. Just then a loud thunderbolt sounded, causing them to pick up their pace. "Don't try to talk right now!" he shouted. "It'll keep 'til we're back at the house!"

They slogged on, half-running now, each moment seeming an eternity to Drewry. Shedding their wet rainwear at the door, Chase led her to the parlor and summoned Bridget to bring them something hot from the kitchen.

"Now," he said, turning his full attention on Drewry, who sat sipping her warm milk, "what's this about your not being Drewry Sheffield?"

"Well, I—I *am* Drewry Sheffield," she said uncomfortably, "but I'm not a nanny by trade."

Chase nodded. "Ah. So that explains it."

Drewry's brow furrowed. Why couldn't he simply be quiet

and let her tell him what a lying deceiver she was? Why did he have to be so kind and warm, and make it so difficult to tell the truth?

"I thought the day we picked you up at the Richmond station you were a bit too . . . refined, shall we say . . . to be a servant girl. Smooth, soft hands. Lovely, well-fitted gowns. A true gentlewoman of breeding, with wit and intelligence . . ."

She couldn't take any more! "Chase, please! I must tell you now, or I fear I'll never find the courage again!"

He chuckled softly. "All right, Drewry dear. I'm sorry. Please, tell me all about your sinful past." He rose to put another log on the fire.

She took a deep breath. He thought she was joking. That whatever she planned to say could be dismissed as the silly ranting of an overwrought female mind. "I lied to you, Chase. I am not the woman the agency sent to care for Sally and Sam."

At that, Chase's head snapped around, his face betraying his confusion.

"I met a girl on the train," Drewry hurried on. "Her name was Suzie. *She* was to be your nanny."

"What became of her?" He returned to his chair and sank into the soft cushion with an expectant look on his face, as if waiting for her explanation to erase any doubt from his mind.

"She got off the train with a soldier she met during the trip. They were to be married in Richmond."

Chase crossed his arms over his chest. "This is a fascinating story, Drewry. Do go on, please." He clamped his jaw and frowned, but he wasn't fooling Drewry. She'd seen that playful gleam in his eye dozens of times when he'd teased Sally and Sam.

He was making fun of her! But Drewry was determined to finish what she had begun. "She told me everything about you—that you would be wearing a blue silk scarf. That your two children would be with you. That you were successful and . . ."

". . . and rich?"

"Yes." She heaved a sigh. What was the use? He probably wouldn't believe anything she said.

"Ah-ha," he said thoughtfully. "I see." He steepled his fingers and studied her face. "Exactly why were you on that southbound train, Drewry?"

Go ahead! Tell it all! she shouted inwardly. *Show him what a worthless human being you really are!* "My uncle, James Sheffield, had been a loving guardian until he went off to fight in the War. He was wounded. After that . . ." *Don't stop now! Go on, or you'll lose your nerve!*

"When he came home," Drewry continued, "his wounds healed, but he took to drinking and playing cards in the saloon. He gambled away practically everything on the farm. And when he ran out of belongings—" she dropped her head, unable to meet his gaze. "He gambled *me."*

Chase inhaled sharply. "Gambled . . . *you?"*

Remembering her promise to Matilda, Drewry lifted her chin then and looked him in the eye. "That's right. Promised me to a horrible old man named Porter Hopkins. So, like a spoiled child, I took the coward's way out. I ran away from home. I didn't know where I'd go, nor what I'd do when I got there. I only knew I could never marry a man I didn't love. Never!"

Drewry cleared her throat, summoning the courage to finish her story. "I got on that train, and when I met Suzie and discovered she had no intention of keeping her bargain with you, I decided to take her place. I really thought it would solve all of our problems . . ." Her voice grew small and soft. "She'd get her handsome soldier, and you'd get your nanny."

There! She'd done it. Drewry stared at the muddy toes of her boots, waiting for a storm of an entirely different kind to break over her head. Chase sat there for the longest time, saying nothing.

Finally, she looked up into his face. Never in all her days had she seen such rage, such fury, such outright anger . . .

Suddenly, he grabbed her shoulders and shook her. "Do you mean to say that . . ." He looked away. Looked to heaven. Looked back into her face, his countenance fierce. "No good, despicable . . ."

She couldn't stay to hear any more. Drewry wrenched herself free and ran up the steps to the sanctuary of her room, leaving Chase alone . . .

Alone with her awful truth!

છે

Drewry slammed her bedroom door so hard, the thud reverberated throughout the room, amplifying the hollowness and desolation she felt inside. Wailing like a child, she flung herself across the bed. The nubby finish of the coverlet felt rough against her hot, tear-stained cheek.

You've lost him! It's over! shouted a desperate voice inside her head. The quiet voice in her heart told her that if she wanted Chase to forgive her, then the man must know what he was forgiving her *for.*

So now he knew . . .

And now *she* knew: He wanted no part of her, of the liar and deceiver she had proven herself to be. His rage had told her that much. He'd even begun to call her names as he'd grasped her shoulders in the vise of his hands. Frightened by the rage she had seen in those near-black irises, she had fled.

Drewry closed her eyes and tried to blot out the hurt and bitter anger that had flooded Chase's face when she revealed the whole sordid truth. *How could I have deceived him? And deceived him for so long? How could he ever trust me again, much less love me?*

But she couldn't block from her mind the image of his handsome face, filled with anguish, then disgust. *How vile I must be in his sight. He probably never wants to lay eyes on me again. Nor can I blame him.* The prospect left her griefstricken. Her throat felt thick, her eyes puffy from crying.

She thought of Suzie with bitterness, wondering if the girl

had found happiness with her soldier, thanks to her part in this deception. But no, it wasn't Suzie's fault. The young woman might have done Chase a terrible injustice by failing to follow through on her contractual agreement to be his children's nanny, but she had never actually deceived him. No. The blame for all that had followed lay at Drewry's doorstep. *It was I—and I alone—who deceived him and lied to him.* And now she was bearing the consequences of those actions—consequences that seemed to include losing Chase forever.

The thought brought a fresh flood of tears. This suffering was of her own doing. So be it. She'd endure Chase's rejection with resignation, as penance for her sin of deceit. Each lonely day that lay ahead would be torture, she knew. Having come so close to true love, she knew what she would be missing—the joy of sharing a silly joke, a trauma, a kiss . . . All those intimate moments were shattered, gone forever.

And it was her own fault.

Still, she had done the right thing in telling Chase the truth. Just as Jeb had promised, the truth *had* set her free. She was free now. Free from the awful burden of secrecy and shame.

Now that her conscience was clear in the sight of her Maker, she could breathe easier. It was enough that she had obeyed her Lord. And even now, she dared to believe—to hope—that somehow, in His infinite mercy, He would bring something good of this heartbreak. God had forgiven her, of that Drewry was quite certain. Was it too much to hope that Chase, too, would find it in his heart to forgive her?

From his reaction, however, it certainly seemed doubtful. Her heart swollen with hurt, Drewry couldn't bring herself to face him again. Confident that he had no wish to see her ever again, she decided to relieve him of that burden. At least she could do *that* right, and she'd do it with dignity!

Quickly, she dried her tears, went to her desk, and rummaged in the drawer for a sheet of stationery. She brought out a piece of her best, rose-scented letter paper and, sick at heart, sat down to write:

> *Magnolia Grange*
> *October 2, 1868*
>
> *Dear Mr. Auburn:*
>   *Due to certain unfortunate circumstances, it is with deepest regret that I must inform you that as of today, I can no longer remain in your employ. Please be assured that these circumstances have nothing whatsoever to do with you personally. I assume all responsibility for the occurrence which has rendered our continued relationship untenable.*
>   *I have nothing but good things to report from my experience with you and your children. You have been more than a mere employer—you have been a friend of the highest caliber. It is with bitter regret that I confess—as I did tonight—that my own character has been found lacking.*
>   *Your high standards will, no doubt, assure you of retaining a more suitable young lady to serve as nanny to Miss Sally and Master Sam. Unless you find it intolerable for me to do so, I will, of course, remain in the household until that replacement has been secured. But I shall fully understand if you would prefer that I leave immediately.*
>
>   *I remain, in all sincerity, your friend,*
>   *Drewry Sheffield*

With trembling hand, Drewry signed her name and returned her pen to its ink pot. She took a sheet of blotting paper and gently pressed it to the feminine script. Then she slipped the letter into a rose-colored envelope and addressed it to Chase.

Heart pounding, she slipped into her houseshoes and silently made her way down the hall. Just as she'd expected, she saw the thin ribbon of light glowing from beneath his library door. Chase Auburn was a man of habit, to be sure. And habits were hard to break.

Honesty, she knew, was one of those habits.

Pausing briefly outside his door, Drewry closed her eyes and prayed. *Dear heavenly Father, I've tried my best to do Your will. Now, all is in Your hands.* The simple words left her with a feeling of quiet assurance, as if God had been waiting for just this prayer. Indeed, Drewry reasoned, if not a single sparrow fell to the ground without His notice, surely He knew about her aching heart and was working in her life now, no matter how bleak things seemed.

Holding her breath, she hunkered down, and, balancing herself, began to slide the envelope under the door as silently as possible. But the space beneath the door was slimmer than she'd reckoned and the letter wouldn't go in easily. It had only half disappeared when the pocket doors whooshed open, the sudden force causing Drewry to lose her balance.

She flung out her arms to steady herself, but instead, she toppled sideways, cracking her head with a sickening *thud* against the wooden door frame.

fifteen

"Drewry? Drewry! Are you all right, my love?"

What was that sound? Why was her head throbbing so? Then she remembered losing her balance, hitting her head . . .

She opened her eyes and found herself lying on the leather couch in Chase's library. Nearby, a lantern glowed brightly, and she drew comfort from the familiarity of the sight.

But there was something else. Was it *love* she heard in Chase's voice?

She dared to look at him and found herself staring straight into dark eyes that seemed filled with shifting stars. Chase's eyes . . . Chase's voice . . .

"Thank God! You've come 'round."

She smiled weakly.

Gently, he wrung out a cloth and dabbed at her face. She gazed into his eyes, trying to read the expression hidden by the room's shadows.

"Does that feel better?" he asked, draping the cloth across her forehead.

She tried to nod.

Intently, he examined one eye, then the other. When he seemed satisfied that she hadn't suffered a concussion, he drew her to him and enclosed her in the strong circle of his arms. Drewry looked longingly into his face, glowing and golden in the soft lamplight.

"It's never going to work, Drewry," he said softly.

Immediately, the pain of the previous hours came crashing in on her. She had assessed the situation correctly, after all, she realized sadly. He was rejecting her. His present actions were only further proof of his Christian kindness. He was concerned for her injury, maybe even felt responsible, but that was all.

"I understand," she whispered. "I plan to leave as soon as possible. Once you've secured my replacement...."

A night shadow crossed his face, momentarily shrouding it with darkness. When the moon illuminated the room once again, Drewry saw tears glistening on his cheeks. Dazed, she reached up and traced their trail down his face.

"No, Drewry. You have it all wrong."

She heard deep undertones of anguish in his voice. "Wrong?" she echoed, hoping against hope.

"Completely. What I mean is—it's not going to work for you to hand in your resignation. I won't accept it."

"Oh?" she squeaked.

Chase let out a long, shuddering sigh. "What a fool I've been. When you confided your secret to me earlier, I . . . well, I'm ashamed to say I lost my temper."

Tenderly he repositioned the cloth on her forehead. "My dear, sweet Drewry. I'm sorry if I frightened you. It's just that I was so consumed with anger at your uncle for his brutal treatment of you—*you* the woman I've come to love with all my heart. And I was angry at *myself* for not being there to protect you. My rage was so great, I was beside myself. Forgive me, my darling."

Drewry blinked, struggling to comprehend the meaning of his words. She'd wanted to hear such a proclamation for so long! Now that he was saying them, she feared that what she was hearing was a result of the blow to her brain. Her head was still pounding, after all, and her vision was blurred . . .

But the love in his voice continued to bathe her. She allowed herself to relax into that love, letting it lap around her in warm waves. She closed her eyes and sank gratefully into that security. She was wanted. She was loved!

"Drewry, listen to me," Chase said softly, brushing stray hairs from her forehead, "my darling, I don't judge you for your deception. You were plunged into such an impossible situation. I don't know what I might have done under similar circumstances. But I know that your intent was never malicious. Please believe me when I say, from the bottom of my heart, there's nothing to forgive."

Nothing?

Drewry couldn't speak. Her heart seemed to be stuck in her throat, making speech impossible.

"I'm afraid, darling," he said at last, his voice husky.

She opened her eyes, and found his dark ones shimmering with unshed tears. "Afraid?" she asked in a whisper. "Afraid of what?"

His sigh echoed throughout the room. "First, I feared loving you. Now, I fear losing you. I'd sooner lose an arm or a leg than lose you, my Lady Nanny. I think I've loved you from the first moment I set eyes on you at the Richmond station. Do you know how crushed I'd have been had you *not* claimed to be the one I'd come to meet?"

"Oh, Chase . . ." With a soft groan, Drewry burrowed into the warm crook between his shoulder and neck. She shivered with delight as his arms tightened around her.

There was one thing she had to know, though. One thing that the rest of her world revolved around. One thing that only he could tell her.

"Chase?"

"Yes, my love."

"After my—my . . . deception . . . how can you ever trust me again?"

"Oh, my darling," he said, gazing at her with such intensity that she trembled. "Don't you see? You proved your love for me when you told me your secret. I've been waiting so very long to share in your life. Waiting so long for your trust in me to grow strong enough to allow you to share it with me."

She blinked in astonishment. "You knew I was hiding something? And you didn't try to find out *what?*" Drewry gulped. "You could have hired a detective . . ."

Chase chuckled. "Perhaps so. But I wanted you to tell me yourself. I sensed that when you loved me enough, you'd tell me."

Drewry sighed. "I wanted to tell you sooner. So many times I almost did. But I was afraid, too. So very much afraid . . ." She shook her head. "Afraid you'd reject me. Afraid you'd hate me . . . But I prayed about it and finally, I told you simply because I loved you too much *not* to."

Chase traced the outline of her jaw with a light brush of his fingertips. "Ah, how can I *not* trust a woman who loves not only me, but also the Lord God, enough to risk telling a painful truth? How can I distrust a love that's willing to be so vulnerable, so trusting?"

"Then . . . you *do* trust me?"

His voice poured over her like liquid music, soothing her, surrounding her, and dissolving all her fears. In that moment, she felt warmer and safer than she'd ever felt before. "My darling Drewry, I trust you completely."

☙

She stood in front of the oval mirror in her room and allowed Matilda to pin a white poinsettia in her hair. "You do makes a lovely bride, Miss Drewry," the older woman said, meeting Drewry's eyes in the mirror. "Mistah Chase be one lucky fella to be gettin' a wife like you."

"Thank you, Matilda." Drewry studied her reflection, seeing the flush of excitement in her cheeks. "And I'm lucky, too."

"Not lucky," Bridget corrected her. "Blessed."

The girl so rarely spoke that the mere sound of her voice stunned Matilda and Drewry into silence. After a moment,

Drewry grasped the girl's hand. "You're so right, Bridget. Luck had nothing to do with it. It was the Good Lord who brought Chase and me together."

"And 'tis the Lord who will *keep* you together," Bridget confirmed with a nod.

Drewry and Matilda exchanged amused glances. "Seems our gal here know as much about the Good Book as anyone," Matilda said with a broad grin.

"You'd best be gettin' downstairs, Miss," the Irish girl interrupted, adjusting Drewry's long, flowing veil. "Pastor Tillman has arrived, and the guests have gathered in the chapel."

The weather had turned unseasonably warm. Even in Richmond, temperatures in the seventies were almost unheard of in December. Drewry knew she had God to thank for that, too.

She tugged at the long, snug sleeves of her white velvet gown, then held them out so that Matilda could fasten the tiny, pearl buttons on each cuff. She secured her mother's cameo at the high stand-up collar of the dress, then picked up her bouquet, which Bridget had fashioned of red roses, white poinsettias, and fresh greenery from Chase's hothouse.

"Well, I'm as ready as I'm ever going to be," she said, her voice trembling.

"Let's go on down, then!" Matilda said.

Out front, Claib was waiting with the carriage. He had polished the chassis until its black enamel gleamed like a black mirror. He cut quite a dashing figure in his long-tailed morning suit, and Drewry told him so.

Bending low at the waist, he swept a gloved hand in front of him. "Your carriage awaits, m'lady," he said, mimicking Pastor Tillman's English butler.

The sounds of laughter and chatter grew louder as Drewry, Bridget, and Matilda rode across the field toward the chapel.

"They're here!" she heard a woman shout. "Start the music!"

a man hollered. "The bride has arrived!"

As the four-piece string ensemble began to play—*something by Beethoven,* she thought—Drewry stood at the end of the path that led to the tiny chapel, marveling at its festive seasonal decorations. The red berries of the holly that trimmed the roof winked merrily at her, and the soft garland of green that trimmed the walls filled the air with the fresh, clean scent of pine. Inside, massive arrangements of white poinsettias and fresh evergreens banked the altar where Chase would soon be waiting . . .

As Drewry remained at the back of the church, ready for the bridal processional to begin, Bridget and Matilda, wearing new frocks, preceded her importantly and found their places in the Auburn pew. Young Sally took up her position, too, prepared to sprinkle rose petals along the path that her new mother's high-topped white boots would take. Beside Sally was little Sam, carrying the white satin pillow cushioning the wedding band. Squirming in his new suit, he grinned up at Drewry.

Scanning the church filled with family and friends, Drewry spotted Uncle James and his lovely Naomi, sitting between her fiancé and her brother-in-law to be, Jeb Sheffield. Missy was seated on Jeb's right. Drewry's family, who turned in their seats like unruly schoolchildren to catch a glimpse of the bride, beamed their approval. She blew them a kiss.

At that moment, the processional began and Pastor Tilton, followed by Chase, emerged from a small room at the side of the church to take their places at the altar.

Chase—resplendent in black suit and tie and starched white shirt, his dark hair gleaming, his eyes searching for hers. Chase—the object of all her hopes and dreams, the promise soon to be fulfilled. Chase—God's special gift to her . . .

Catching her eye, he mouthed the words, "I love you."

She answered him with a smile and a wink.

And that—their silent, "for-our-eyes-only" dialogue seemed to convey—is no bluff!

A Letter To Our Readers

Dear Reader:

In order that we might better contribute to your reading enjoyment, we would appreciate your taking a few minutes to respond to the following questions. When completed, please return to the following:

Rebecca Germany, Editor
Heartsong Presents
P.O. Box 719
Uhrichsville, Ohio 44683

1. Did you enjoy reading *Drewry's Bluff*?
   ❑ Very much. I would like to see more books
      by this author!
   ❑ Moderately
      I would have enjoyed it more if _____

      _____

2. Are you a member of **Heartsong Presents**? ❑Yes ❑No
   If no, where did you purchase this book?_____

   _____

3. What influenced your decision to purchase this
   book? (Check those that apply.)

   ❑ Cover   ❑ Back cover copy

   ❑ Title   ❑ Friends

   ❑ Publicity   ❑ Other_____

4. How would you rate, on a scale from 1 (poor) to 5
   (superior), **Heartsong Presents'** new cover design?_____

5. On a scale from 1 (poor) to 10 (superior), please rate the following elements.

    ___ Heroine   ___ Plot

    ___ Hero   ___ Inspirational theme

    ___ Setting   ___ Secondary characters

6. What settings would you like to see covered in **Heartsong Presents** books? _____

_____

_____

7. What are some inspirational themes you would like to see treated in future books? _____

_____

_____

8. Would you be interested in reading other **Heartsong Presents** titles?   ❑ Yes   ❑ No

9. Please check your age range:
   ❑ Under 18   ❑ 18-24   ❑ 25-34
   ❑ 35-45   ❑ 46-55   ❑ Over 55

10. How many hours per week do you read? _____

Name _____

Occupation _____

Address _____

City _____ State _____ Zip _____

Classic Fiction for a New Generation

Pollyanna
and
Pollyanna Grows Up

*Eleanor H. Porter's classic stories of an extraordinary
girl who saw the good in everyone. . . and made
everyone feel good about themselves.*

___*Pollyanna*— An orphan dutifully taken in by her repressive
aunt, the well-heeled Miss Polly Harrington, Pollyanna Whittier
reinvents a game of her father's and finds a way to hide her tears.
No one can resist Pollyanna for long and soon almost everyone
is playing "the Glad Game," everyone except Aunt Polly.
BTP-65 $2.97

___*Pollyanna Grows Up*—Ruth Carew's refined Boston world
has just been turned upside down. The reason, of course, is
obvious: Pollyanna Whittier has come to visit. From Boston to
Beldingsville to Europe and back again, *Pollyanna Grows Up*
continues the adventures of an irrepressible American girl on
the brink of womanhood at the turn of the century. In everything
she does—especially the Glad Game—Pollyanna reflects the
boundless love of her Heavenly Father. BTP-80 $2.97

Heart♥ng

·········Presents·········

*Temporarily out of stock.

Great Inspirational Romance at a Great Price!

Heartsong Presents books are inspirational romances in contemporary and historical settings, designed to give you an enjoyable, spirit-lifting reading experience. You can choose from 148 wonderfully written titles from some of today's best authors like Colleen L. Reece,

When ordering quantities less than twelve, above titles are $2.95 each.

SEND TO: Heartsong Presents Reader's Service
P.O. Box 719, Uhrichsville, Ohio 44683

Please send me the items checked above. I am enclosing $_____.
(please add $1.00 to cover postage per order. OH add 6.25% tax. NJ add 6%). Send check or money order, no cash or C.O.D.s, please.
To place a credit card order, call 1-800-847-8270.

NAME _____

ADDRESS _____

CITY/STATE_____ ZIP _____

HPS NOV.

Heartsong Presents
Love Stories Are Rated G!

That's for godly, gratifying, and of course, great! If you love a thrilling love story, but don't appreciate the sordidness of some popular paperback romances, **Heartsong Presents** is for you. In fact, **Heartsong Presents** is the *only inspirational romance book club*, the only one featuring love stories where Christian faith is the primary ingredient in a marriage relationship.

Sign up today to receive your first set of four, never before published Christian romances. Send no money now; you will receive a bill with the first shipment. You may cancel at any time without obligation, and if you aren't completely satisfied with any selection, you may return the books for an immediate refund!

Imagine...four new romances every four weeks—two historical, two contemporary—with men and women like you who long to meet the one God has chosen as the love of their lives...all for the low price of $9.97 postpaid.

To join, simply complete the coupon below and mail to the address provided. **Heartsong Presents** romances are rated G for another reason: They'll arrive *Godspeed!*